THE DARK AT THE BOTTOM OF THE STAIRS

Ruth's eyes fell on the patterns the candlelight traced on the walls. They were bizarre and erratic in movement. *Of course they're moving, you damned fool. Your hand is trembling. This is the most frightened you've ever been. Think of it as a first, as an experience. Someday that's all you'll think of this as: an experience.* But then there was a dreadful crooning sound, and after a moment she realized it had escaped from her lips. She was close to fainting; fear was paralyzing her. She had to go on. Before she crumpled, fell into a swoon, and tumbled down the stairs. She set her foot on the step below, then stepped off with her other foot. And then she saw . . .

She wanted to scream, tried to scream, but nothing would come. Coming toward her . . . coming toward her. . . . There was no hope, none at all. She couldn't scream, couldn't move. . . . *For God's sake, please . . . please!* . . . *Mom . . . Mommmmm. . . .*

QUANTITY SALES

Most Dell books are available at special quantity discounts when purchased in bulk by corporations, organizations, and special-interest groups. Custom imprinting or excerpting can also be done to fit special needs. For details write: Dell Publishing, 666 Fifth Avenue, New York, NY 10103. Attn.: Special Sales Department.

INDIVIDUAL SALES

Are there any Dell books you want but cannot find in your local stores? If so, you can order them directly from us. You can get any Dell book in print. Simply include the book's title, author, and ISBN number if you have it, along with a check or money order (no cash can be accepted) for the full retail price plus $2.00 to cover shipping and handling. Mail to: Dell Readers Service, P.O. Box 5057, Des Plaines, IL 60017.

EVIL

Richard O'Brien

A DELL BOOK

Published by
Dell Publishing
a division of
The Bantam Doubleday Dell
Publishing Group, Inc.
666 Fifth Avenue
New York, New York 10103

ISBN: 0-440-20226-4

Printed in the United States of America

Published simultaneously in Canada

January 1989

10 9 8 7 6 5 4 3 2 1

KRI

To Mary Ann

EVIL

1

"Let's visit Raymond's grave."

Someone—later, no one could remember who —had made the suggestion. Right away they'd gone for it. After all, it was an evening for sentiment: fifteen years since they'd graduated, and all that. The band was still playing "The Last Dance" as, a little drunk, they straggled out of the gym. There were seven of them.

Seven of them now, as there had been seven of them then. Karen St. Germain slowed her pace, allowing her to study the others as they drifted past her.

Her eye fell on her husband. Still blond and rugged, Buddy was talking to Matt Menard in his usual breezy, self-assured manner. Matt had always been the oddball among them; the super-brain who was drawn to the blue-collar world.

Back then a red-hot car jockey tooling around in a souped-up junker, today he was a name of some sort on the race-car circuit.

Ruth Kascyk's sharp glance swept over Karen like shears cutting away a garment. Like old times, Karen thought wryly to herself. How often in the past had Ruth, with a single look, known exactly what she was up to and stripped her bare? The two exchanged tight, knowing smiles, and then both found themselves distracted by Tim Cober.

Tim had stumbled against Eve, and instantly, as if by long-trained instinct, tried to erase the moment with a grin and a gag. Still the class clown, Karen noted; still unable to relax and let his innate likability make up for the joke of a body he'd been given: short, round, and looking over-fleshed no matter how fiercely he'd exercised, no matter how agonizingly he'd dieted. And Eve's reaction to his cover-up was the same as it would have been fifteen years before: a soft, tender smile of understanding and acceptance.

Eve Daw, with her slightly-too-wide shoulders and air of gentleness. How many boys had Karen seen gaze wistfully at Eve as they passed her in those long-ago school corridors? Boys too old to be comfortable with their mother, longing in-stead for Eve to take their head upon her lap, run her fingers through their hair . . .

And Sam Buhl . . . Karen's gaze found him and quickly fell away, just as it had all that evening. Sam, the newcomer, the emigrant from what, to the rest of them back then, had been the exotic, faraway, almost unimaginable world of New York City. Here he was, still with them in the way he'd always been with them: of them and yet, somehow . . . apart.

The mid-October night they stepped into came almost like a blow; unexpectedly mild, oddly oppressive. Karen glanced up at the placard that hung limply above the building's entrance: EVERTON HIGH SCHOOL—CLASS OF 1974. Four days of driving rain had ended late the night before, yet everything was still damp. The cardboard sign had buckled, beads of moisture clung to it, and an odd scent hung in the air. It took Karen a moment to place it. "Am I out of my mind," she asked, "or do I really smell the ocean?" They were almost sixty miles from the sea.

It had been clear from the start of the evening that Ruth was still the quickest of the group. She leapt in now. "You're right. I wonder what it could be."

A bank of floodlights loomed behind them, throwing Sam's angular features into shadow. "Can't imagine," he said.

Buddy laughed, and Karen's stare—after a brief hesitation—left Sam and settled on her husband. Buddy's blond hair and white teeth glinted in the light. "Hey, you've not only been away from New Jersey too long," he observed dryly.

"You obviously never were here long *enough*. In our fair state there isn't a smell you don't come across somewhere along the way, a few of them even natural. God only knows what this one is." He turned to the others. "If you aging relics want, you can all cram in with us. Karen and I came in the wagon—the BMW's in the shop again."

Tim grinned up at the two women who stood near him. "The BMW's in the shop again," he mocked. "What sadder words of tongue or pen?"

As the seven headed toward the station wagon, Karen turned to Sam. "You sit up front with Buddy and me," she told him, her voice calm and certain, her eyes less so. Sam's reply was a nod.

The smell of the ocean is supposed to be bracing, Karen told herself. Instead, she found it disconcerting. Like a lot of things tonight, it was unexpected, out of place. The scent of brine, the unseasonably mild air, the *heaviness* of it, Sam's unexpected appearance . . . and Eve's behavior. As they reached the car she turned and glanced back at Eve. In her quiet way, Eve was—had always been—the prettiest of the three women. Her figure was still softly attractive, and the feeling she'd always conveyed—of warmth, even of sanctuary—was unchanged. But tonight, even before their first drink, she'd been oddly boisterous, even reckless. Eve was married, had two children—the only one of the women with children—but she'd come all the way from Ohio without her husband. "Couldn't find a baby-sit-ter" had been her offhand explanation. Now as four of them crowded into the backseat she shouted a little too gaily, "Just room for three. So I call Matt's lap!"

Others were leaving the reunion, and as Buddy slid the key into the ignition, some of their old classmates began drifting past. Two of the women waved to Buddy. "So long, Golden Boy!" they called. Wryly, he waved back and started the car. He pulled forward a few feet, then made a sweeping turn.

Eve's body jerked upright. "Wrong direction!" she sang out. "The cemetery's back there." As she'd promised, she was on Matt's lap. Ruth was sandwiched between Matt and Tim.

Buddy laughed. "That's why you didn't make valedictorian, babe. Never did have the memory."

"What does that mean?"

"It means you don't remember about Raymond. That his family was from Hinnsville originally. That's where they buried him. Come back to you now, salutatorian?"

"Why should it?"

"You were at the funeral."

"No I wasn't."

"Buddy's right," Karen called back over her shoulder.

"I was *not* at the funeral," Eve insisted.

"Of course you were," Ruth broke in, her darkly handsome good looks showing impatience. "Don't you remember? We *all* showed up. Well, the five of us anyway. Sam and Matt had already gone off to seek their fortunes. Anyway, there we were, the five of us. But the interesting thing about it was that we all showed up separately. And when we saw each other, we all got this terribly *uncomfortable* look on our faces."

Eve shrugged. Obviously she still didn't remember.

The conversation faded away and out of Karen's mind as her thoughts turned to the man beside her. *Dammit,* she swore to herself while she stared into the blackness ahead. *Unfinished business, that's all it is.*

As the station wagon sped along the deserted streets there was a stir in the back seat. "Have some," Eve was urging Matt. She'd grabbed a bottle of Scotch from a table as they left the gym. Matt shook his head. "Had enough," he told her, turning his face to the window.

"Never knew you to have enough in the old days. From what I heard, you never got enough of *anything* in the old days," Eve teased. Matt shrugged and looked uncomfortable.

The suddenness of it almost made Buddy duck. One instant the station wagon was speeding down a ribbon of gauzy black; the next it was caught in a maelstrom. Sheets of rain pounded against the windshield; an avalanche of wind rocked the car.

"Typhoon!" Eve cried out merrily.

"It could be a hurricane," Ruth said sharply. "There were warnings all day."

"Come on! A hurricane here? This far from the shore?" Buddy called back to her as he struggled with the wheel.

"Ruth's right about the warnings." Karen raised her voice above the storm. "I heard them, too. Just didn't pay any attention."

"Don't blame you," Matt contributed. "No reason to start slapping boards across your windows. Like Buddy said, we're too far out in the boonies."

"That's what they whistled in Connecticut back in 1938," Tim offered amiably. "Until it hit," he concluded. "Wham-o!"

"Connecticut's near water," Buddy answered.

Tim shrugged. "I've got a feeling it caught them all the way in. But I could be wrong." He shook his head as Eve silently offered him the Scotch. "I've attained the perfect buzz," he told her. "One more degree of buzz and I start throwing up."

"Jesus!" A huge branch flew across the car's hood. Instinctively Buddy swerved to the right, then, adrenaline pumping through him, found himself battling to keep the car on the road.

"Piece of cake," he muttered dryly a moment later, finally regaining control. Then he found himself flinching as something hurtled against the side of the car. From the sound and the vibrations it set off, it had been large and heavy. Buddy

pictured the dent and the scarred paint. The
Volvo was three years old, but he was proud of
the shape it was in.

"Out comes the BMW and in goes this one,"
Karen muttered humorously. "Bound to stop
soon," she added reassuringly.

"Not if it's a hurricane," Ruth said. "Why don't
you try the radio, Buddy?"

He popped it on and tapped the scan button
simultaneously. Reception in these hills was always a problem. On a night like this it would
certainly be worse. "Is it moving?" he asked
Karen after a few seconds went by, unwilling to
take his eyes off the road. All he heard was static.

She didn't understand at first, then looked
down. The dial was floating all the way to the
right, then back to the left, then starting to the
right again. "It's moving, but it's not getting anything," she told him.

He raised the volume, but it didn't help. "Cut
off from the world," he sang out, in what he
hoped sounded like a cheerful, carefree voice. No
sense worrying anyone, especially yourself, he
thought while the steering wheel vibrated in his
hands. He'd never driven through anything like
this. He was tempted to pull to the side of the
road; even at their full speed, the wipers were
barely doing the job. But with all the debris flying
through the air, it hardly seemed safe. The roads
around here were lined with trees; nothing like
stopping for safety and then having an oak topple

on you. As a child he'd once seen what a falling tree could do to a car and the people inside.

Besides, if he kept driving, he might outrun it. Could be it was only a squall; he'd run into a few of them before. Half a mile away everything was probably calm and dry. Tim and Ruth had to be wrong; they were too far inland for a hurricane. He'd lived here all his life; there'd never been one, nothing close to one. He glanced at Karen, but her face was turned away. She was talking to Sam. He couldn't hear her over the noise of the storm, but she looked calm enough.

"You hadn't told your aunt and uncle, either," Karen was saying to Sam. "I mean, about leaving right after graduation."

"Don't imagine they worried." Sam shrugged.

"No, they didn't worry," she told him. "You took hardly any of your things. I know"—her voice fell to almost a whisper—"I went over there."

"Wasn't much to take."

"Even the picture of your family—I remember you once told me it was the only one you had of your parents and brother. You left that behind, too."

He didn't say anything, and she stared up at him, wishing she could see his face more clearly; read it. Was he thinking what she was? No, you didn't take the photo of your family with you, but what about my picture? It wasn't there, left behind with the rest of your things. What about *my* picture?

He'd always been like this. Quiet, always off a little somewhere. One of the things that had attracted her to him. Attracted and infuriated. Like now. She tried again. "What about your mother?"

"What about her?"

"Is she still alive? Do you see her?"

"Yes. She lives with my brother and his wife. Sometimes I see her. Not for long. Not often."

"It wasn't her fault she couldn't keep the two of you after your father died."

"I know. But it . . . it changed things. Not just for me. For her, too."

She gazed into the swirling night, her eyes registering none of it. "I'm glad you came," she told him, not knowing till she said it that it was true.

"Hey!" It was a shout, and it came from both Tim and Matt. Rain was exploding into the car. Eve had started to roll down the window. Matt, his big hand tight over hers, rolled it back up. "No one wanted the Scotch," Eve explained lightly, "so I thought I'd toss it."

"Open that window again and I'll toss *you*," Matt told her gruffly, grabbing the bottle with one hand and wiping the rain off his face with the other.

"I'd like that," she answered, smiling down at him.

"You ever see anything like this?" Buddy called to Sam.

"Maybe. A couple of times. But it was different. At sea. No tree branches whizzing past me."

"At sea." So he'd been at sea. Karen found herself wondering what his life had been like since he'd left Everton. Again she stared at his left hand. No ring, no sign of one. Not that that necessarily meant anything, not these days.

The storm wasn't letting up. Again something thunked and scratched against the car. Another branch, Buddy thought, wondering what the wagon would look like when they were out of this; probably a mess. Something to get annoyed about tomorrow. Just now he was simply grateful that nothing more had happened. Grateful, too, that so far they hadn't encountered a car, not even one, behind them. Enough danger just being alone in the middle of all this.

Damn. Buddy's fingers squeezed the wheel. He hadn't seen the bridge until it was too late. Couldn't hit the brakes now, might skid. Probably no reason to stop. But the wind drove the rain so hard that it looked as if the river itself was sweeping across the bridge.

As he began to roll over the timbers he felt the car slip sideways, and he realized he'd seen it right: the bridge *was* awash.

Matt and Eve were on the driver's side of the car. "Careful, Buddy," Matt called, "you're almost up against the side of the bridge!"

"Can't help it!" Buddy answered, the tendons

in his hands straining as he gripped the wheel. "This damn bus is floating!"

He'd heard about things like this, read about them. People trying to drive across a bridge, being pushed against the side railings, the railings giving way . . .

The voices around him seemed unconcerned.

"You're scraping paint. Good thing this isn't the BMW!"

"This baby got oars?"

Then he felt it. Traction. The tires seemed to be making contact again. For an instant they faltered, and then it was all right; the car began to creep forward. A few thousand points for front-wheel drive, he found himself thinking. A cheer went up and he relaxed . . . a little. They were free.

"May and Irene got it right—back there in the parking lot!" Eve's voice rang out. " 'Golden Boy.' That's what you are, what you always were! A little thing like a giant hurricane's not going to stop our Buddy!"

He barely heard. He knew they had to be close to the cemetery, and strained to see ahead. A few thousands points, too, to the genius who came up with the idea of putting white lines on the road. Be lost without them.

Karen saw the sign first. "Here we are!" she called. As Buddy pulled over, rushing water at the side of the road hissed against the tires.

Without the sign they'd never have found it, not in this weather. The cemetery was nothing but a low stone wall around a small group of tombstones. Couldn't be more than a couple of hundred buried here, Buddy thought. If that.

"Looks like we're going to have to pay our respects from here," Karen suggested, addressing all of them. "I mean, it's too dangerous out there, isn't it?"

As if in answer, something smashed down onto the hood, then, storm-driven, skidded off it.

"Pretty goddam dangerous *in*, too," Tim chirruped. "Let's give our dear departed classmate a wave, a respectful nod, the symbolic hug to end all symbolic hugs, and then let's get the hell out of here."

"Poor Raymond," Ruth said. "Think of it. All these years. All these years that we've been alive. When he should have been alive, too. Cheated out of all these years."

They fell silent. The wind-whipped station wagon shuddered.

Finally Buddy turned to them. "Okay?" he asked. When one or two of them nodded, and no one disagreed, he pulled slowly back onto the road, then continued in the same direction as before. "Don't want to chance that bridge," he explained. "This should get us back to the highway. Might also give us more protection. I seem to remember it's between hills part of the way. Sheltered."

They had driven only three quarters of a mile when the white line disappeared; the pike they'd been traveling on had become a narrow country road. Buddy cursed softly to himself. The storm was no better here, and without the white lines it was almost impossible to see ahead.

Since leaving the cemetery, they'd all been silent. Ruth's voice, when she spoke, had an odd tone to it. "No one's saying anything," she commented. "Could our silence have anything to do with guilt?"

There was a shifting of bodies. Finally Tim asked, "Guilt about what?"

"You know. *Raymond.* About *that night.*"

"Hard to get too choked up," Matt muttered.

"What do you mean?"

"Hard to feel much of anything about such a wimp."

"A nerd," Tim corrected, amused.

"No," Eve contradicted them, her voice low and serious. "He wasn't a wimp. He wasn't a nerd."

"What was he then?"

There was a pause, and then she told them. "A creep."

"A creep!" Tim's voice was a startled giggle. "Hey, isn't there some kind of rule about not speaking ill of the dead?"

Eve bowed her head. "The fact is, there was something very unpleasant about Raymond."

They looked at each other, puzzled, uneasy.

All but Ruth. She wasn't letting it rest. "Wasn't he a foster child?" she asked. "Or adopted?"

"Seems to me he came from a large family. Poor," Tim said. "But I could be wrong."

"I don't think we know much about him," Karen told them. "Probably never did. I've been going through the yearbook lately. You know, because of the reunion. Raymond was on the 'camera shy' page. No picture, no activities listed, either. Just nothing."

"Jesus Christ!" The words exploded out of Tim.

"What's wrong?" Buddy called, tightly. The last two miles had been even worse; he'd been plowing through debris; shattered branches blanketed the road.

"A real mother of a tree! Just came down behind us. If this bus'd been a second slower, we'd all be flatter than a transvestite without falsies. Hope you weren't thinking of hanging a U and doubling back. The county road boys are going to have a job clearing away that baby."

Buddy hadn't been thinking of turning back. He didn't much want to go forward, either. What he yearned to do was stop. The frenzy of the storm, having to battle its wildness while straining to see ahead, was beginning to unnerve him.

"Do you realize we haven't passed a house in miles?" Ruth asked suddenly.

"Maybe we just can't see them—power failure —no lights," Eve suggested.

"No," Matt told her, "Ruth's right. There just

about aren't any houses. It's pretty much deserted all along the way."

"I don't remember this road at all," Tim said, shrugging.

"Runs into Thirty-one," Matt answered. "Not too much to it. Just scraggy woods, a brook or two. Used to be gravel part of the way. A bitch in the winter. Good fishing along the river, though. You hit the river just before Thirty-one."

There was a whistling sound, and the car seemed for an instant to be airborne. "Damn!" Buddy cried. No question now. He'd never been through anything like this in his life.

"Tough driving," Sam told him. "I don't envy you." Buddy said nothing, his eyes intent on the road. Beside him, Karen stirred.

"Look!" she said, pointing past Sam. There were lights off to the right.

"Well, *someone* lives in this godforsaken place," Tim commented. "Anyone know who it is?"

"I remember the house," Matt said. "Sort of up on a hill. Used to be the only one on the road. Guess it still is. Never did know who lived there, though." No one else said anything.

Buddy kept driving, fighting to see ahead. Each time the wind hurled something against the car, or across it, he found himself wincing. Twice his tires squealed, and he realized he'd blundered into the gravel that bordered the road and was headed into the embankment just beyond. Though he recovered quickly and steered out of trouble both times, he found himself shaken. How much of it had been luck? How would he do the next time? They were barely going thirty-five, but even at that speed . . . Then, abruptly, he took his foot off the gas pedal and a moment later braked. "The way the headlights are reflecting is weird," he announced. "Sit tight. I'm going to take a look."

He pushed down on the door handle, then found himself battling to open the door. The wind was hitting the wagon broadside. Its power was extraordinary. Finally he got his shoulder into the door, took advantage of a momentary shift of the wind, and slid out. Immediately the wind tore the door out of his hands, slamming it shut. As bad as the storm had seemed in the confines of the car, its brutality caught him unprepared. It flung him back against the Volvo, the rain slamming at his face. He raised his arms to protect himself, then, bent low, forced his way forward. As he moved alongside the beams of the headlights, he began to suspect what they were picking up.

Another few seconds and he was sure. The river Matt had spoken of had to be flooding. A gust of wind caught him and spun him to the ground, his hands and knees scraping against gravel. Raising his head, his hands cupped around his face to keep the rain out of his eyes, he squinted ahead into the gloom, trying to find a way of judging the water's depth.

Finally he saw it. That must be what it is, he told himself, marveling. One of those yellow signs signifying an approaching curve. Only the top half was visible. *Jesus! That deep.* Bracing himself, he turned, and in a half crouch made his way back to the others.

Before he could open the door, Karen and Matt had to push against it while he pulled. Soaked through, exhausted, he fell back against the seat. "Can't go forward. That's a goddam *ocean* out there. If Tim's right about that tree, we can't go back, either. We'll have to ask the people at the house to put us up." He shifted into reverse and carefully fed in gas. The backup lights would be of limited use. "Let me know if I'm going off," he called to those in back, "assuming *you* can see anything."

Twice he had to stop and pull forward, then, as Matt directed him, continue back along the road. The distance was short, but the combination of the weather, the visibility, and an unknown road made the driving agony, even embarrassing, as he backed and filled like a beginner. Finally he heard Matt shout, "You got it! You're past the driveway!"

It was almost over. Soon he'd be able to stop. Buddy felt relief flood through him as he turned up the drive. Already the driving was easier, now that the wind was at his back. When, a few yards on, he saw the huge branch blocking the way, he shrugged it off. Even if they couldn't move it, the house was only a short run from here.

Buddy started to jerk on the hand brake, but Sam stopped him. "My turn," he insisted.

The headlights caught Sam as he staggered out in front of the car, fighting to keep his balance as the wind tore at him. The branch was huge and heavy, and twice he sprawled across it, tossed by the storm. The contrast was almost grotesque; Sam's desperate struggle, against a backdrop of the serene orange-yellow lights of their imminent shelter.

"Are you all right?" Karen asked as Sam ducked back onto the seat beside her. She didn't seem to mind that he was drenched through. Buddy grimaced. She hadn't asked him how *he* was. And she'd drawn away from his sodden clothing.

2

Moments later they drew up to the front steps.
Every light in the house was on. "We may be in
luck. Looks like they're partying," Tim announced cheerfully. The original high spirits of
the group had been dampened by the drive; now
the promised sanctuary of the house revived
them. There had been some laughter as they
pushed their way out of the car.

The laughter changed to gasps as the wind and
rain caught them. Within seconds they were
soaked through. Ruth seized Sam's arm. "Do you
think we'll make it?" They were already at the
foot of the stairs, but she was only half kidding.

Behind her, Eve lost her footing and suddenly
found herself blown against the side of the front
porch. Tim leapt forward to help her. As he
reached for her, his hand slid across her breast.

"First time ever. After how many dates?" he shouted as he helped her up, but she didn't seem to know what he was talking about.

By the time Eve and Tim had fought their way on to the porch, Buddy was already pounding on the door. The others huddled together, the wind shrieking around them, the rain like darts wherever flesh was exposed. When no one responded, Buddy tried again, this time using both fists. "Maybe they can't hear us," he shouted. "The noise."

Sam brushed past him and tried the door. It opened. His hand on the latch, he looked back at them. In turn they glanced at each other. Then they shrugged. In weather like this it was foolish to stand on ceremony. They crowded in quickly, and then, a few feet inside the hallway, stopped. Buddy and Sam, after a brief battle with the wind, their backs straining against the door, closed it.

"God, what a relief," Ruth exclaimed.

The house was a Victorian, huge, with a long, wide, high-ceilinged center hall. Doors opened off to each side. Halfway down the entry hall a staircase led to the second floor. Almost all the lights were on, but they were of considerably lower wattage than they'd seemed from outside. Poor farm people, Karen thought as she took in her surroundings, noticing the peeling wallpaper, the worn wood flooring that was erratically masked by equally worn carpets. Then she jumped as Ruth shouted, *"Hello!"*

They waited for a reply, but none came. Buddy cupped his hands around his mouth and tried. "Hey! Anyone here? . . . Sorry to barge in, but . . ."

The only answer was a slight humming sound that seemed to come from beneath their feet. "There must be someone here," Karen said. "All these lights . . ."

Tim nodded. He seemed uneasy. "Might be out back. In a barn, tending to the livestock," he offered.

"Everyone in the house?" Ruth asked, her tone supercilious.

"Emergency situation." Tim shrugged, not looking at her.

Sam shook his head. "No sense just standing here," he told them. "Might as well scout around."

Sam moved in one direction, Buddy in another. Alone, Karen walked to the back of the house, where she thought she might find the kitchen. The lights seemed to be flickering. The house smelled musty. The howling of the wind and the frantic tattoo of the rain were unnervingly loud. Somewhere a loose shutter banged.

Sam and Ruth found themselves in the living room, a massive square with a twenty-foot ceiling, its walls streaked by years of grime. Despite

the lamplight the room was gloomy, the furniture
threadbare and scuffed. Ruth found herself wondering about their hosts. They could be simple
farm people, warm and glad to help. Or they
could be something else. She glanced at Sam. Fifteen years had changed him. His face was thinner
now, almost gaunt, and his still-muscular frame
seemed leaner. But that look in his eye hadn't
changed, that look that always seemed to be seeing just beyond . . . She'd hoped from the beginning that Sam would be at the reunion. Otherwise, she might not have gone.

As for the rest, how many of the others still
mattered? Only this little group tonight. And
even of them, how many counted now? Tim had
never been more than amusing; Buddy and Matt
ex-lovers of short duration—she'd never really
missed them once they were gone. And as for
Karen and Eve . . . Eve had become so hope-
lessly domestic, and Karen . . . Well, Karen was
still her best friend. They still corresponded, even
called each other occasionally. Karen was making
her way into a career, starting as a secretary,
working into public relations, so they had that in
common . . . but when it came down to it,
Karen was her best friend by default. Ruth's circle in New York was bright, brittle, never ventur-
ing much beyond the surface; they were really
not much more than acquaintances. Funny—
with all the planning she'd done, all the plotting
out of her life, she'd never once thought to plan

for other people. . . . She turned toward Sam and placed a hand on his arm. But before she had a chance to speak, the silence was torn by a scream. And then another.

"Karen!" Sam turned and ran out of the room, Ruth close behind him.

When they reached Karen she was in Buddy's arms. She seemed to be in shock, her eyes huge, unfocused.

"What's wrong?" Sam asked as the others ran up. Buddy shook his head. Moaning, Karen pointed toward the kitchen door.

It was the swinging kind. Sam pushed it open and let it swing back almost instantly, but was too late. The others had seen.

"My God," Ruth gasped. Eve stifled a cry and averted her face. Tim had gone white; Matt's face tightened.

Buddy led Karen back to the living room. As the others trailed behind, Sam wondered if any of them had noticed the rest of it.

Karen collapsed onto the couch, moaning. She couldn't force the scene out of her mind: the middle-aged man and woman sprawled upon what had been an ordinary kitchen floor, now a sea of crimson. She could still see their limbs, grotesquely frozen in tortured horror, the chilling masks of faces caught in their final agonies. The blood-spattered walls, the violent valleys of flesh, torn at, split apart, over and over . . . She shut her eyes tightly and pressed her hands down hard against the cushions as she tried to force the image from her mind. But it did no good; she saw it all again, clear, savagely clear.

When she heard Sam's voice she seized on it and turned to him. He was at the phone, looking at the others and shaking his head. "The line must be down," he said as he returned the receiver to its cradle. He flicked on a radio. Nothing but static. Then tried the beat-up old TV set. Static again, and a flickering empty screen.

Buddy's voice was strained. "We've got to let the police know," he murmured. Karen turned her face toward the back of the couch, suddenly overwhelmed by fear. She'd never be able to go to sleep again without dread—afraid of what her dreams would be, inescapable visions of torn, bloodied flesh. . . .

"Buddy and I could drive back as far as the tree Tim saw come down," Sam said. "Maybe we can drive around it; if not, we might be able to move it."

"And if we can't, we could hoof it the rest of the way—provided the bridge isn't out," Buddy finished.

"I think we should all go," Ruth said flatly.

"It's dangerous out there," Buddy warned. "The wind . . ."

"My guess is we'd all prefer the danger to . . . this," Ruth told him. "Or am I wrong?"

From her tone it was obvious she expected none of them to disagree. No one did.

3

As she stepped through the door Karen realized she'd already half forgotten how bad it was out here. The wind battered her, and the rain was like a million tiny razorblades, slicing, nicking her hands and face. The driver's door was next to the stairs; she slid in that way, not wanting to spend another moment in this storm. Sam had already struggled in from the passenger side. The others fought their way into the backseat. Rain streamed down their clothing and puddled on the floor. Buddy jumped in, then bent over the wheel, trying to hear the engine. "All this water; she may not start," he said, turning the key again. It took three more tries before the engine sparked and caught. Slowly, the relief showing on his face, Buddy guided the station wagon down the rutted driveway. The glow of the house's lights fell over their shoulders. No one looked back.

Eve couldn't think of anything more grotesque, finding herself back on Matt's lap after what they'd just been through. Matt found the Scotch on the floor, took a pull, and offered it to her. She took a quick swallow and then passed the bottle to Ruth. Eventually, everyone in the car but Buddy had a drink. They'd all needed it.

Eve shook her head. "I've never seen anything so horrible."

Matt grimaced. "I've seen a few like that, kind of. On the speedways. Not the same kind of thing, of course. Those were accidents."

"Terrible." Ruth shuddered. "How can you keep on racing if it means you have to keep facing that kind of horror?"

"It's what I do," Matt told her flatly, matter-of-factly. "It comes with the territory."

Buddy was beginning to wonder if they'd made the right decision. He'd felt immense relief on leaving the house, but now as he struggled to find his way back along the road he was having second thoughts. There was horror back there, but it was over. Out here it could happen again, at any moment, and happen to *them*. He'd slowed to a crawl, but it was a wonder a branch, caught by the wind, hadn't already smashed through one of the windows, shattering bones, tearing flesh. If only this damned rain would slacken so that he could see . . . Then, abruptly, he slammed his foot down on the brake.

He was on the lee side of the wind this time; his door opened without difficulty, while on the passenger side Sam struggled with his. As he stepped onto the road, Buddy involuntarily cried out. It *was* water again. It was ice-cold and reached all the way to his ankles. The wind tore at him viciously as he straightened up; there were no hills here; the storm came at him with full power. Awed, he crouched against the side of the car. Then he noticed. He hadn't moved a step, yet the water had risen inches higher. For the first time he was aware of the frightening roar of rushing water. A dam must have burst. Something smashed against his leg, hurled by the flood. It was coming at them very, very quickly.

"Out!" Sam was yelling. Karen pushed past him, and then, as Sam reached for the handle of the rear door, she found herself picked up, whirled, and knocked flat by the wind. As she struggled to rise, she realized she was yards away from the car and being carried by a swift-moving current. "Sam!" she cried, stretching out her arms.

She couldn't see anything but the lights of the car, receding as she struggled against the flood. Even though the water was not much more than waist-deep, its power was extraordinary; no matter how hard she battled, it kept pushing her back.

Then a loud splash, and she felt a grip on her wrist. Her cry of relief was cut short as she realized that whoever had caught her was being swept away, too. The water was ice. She cried out in pain and fright, her legs and free arm flailing, frantically seeking something, anything, a foothold, a handhold. . . .

Then she stopped short, halted by the hand that gripped her. "Come on!" a voice rang out. It was Sam. He'd managed to anchor himself somehow.

The current was just as bad here, but with Sam bracing her, she was able to jam her left foot against something—a rock probably. With her other foot she sought another hold. She found it; and then slowly, painfully, they fought their way through the water; Sam moving ahead, setting himself; she catching up to him; Sam pushing forward again, struggling against the water as they inched their way toward the station wagon.

It seemed to go on for hours; and then, miraculously, they reached the car, its still-burning lights giving it the appearance of a haven. The water was above their waists now. As she held on to a door handle, recovering, she felt the Volvo begin to give way, to bob, as the flood started to lift it. Terror-stricken, she stared at Sam. The surface beneath their feet was the road; smooth and flat, it would give them nothing to hook onto. By the time they were carried back to where they'd begun their struggle, they'd be moving too quickly and the water would be too deep; there'd be far less chance this time of catching hold, of saving themselves. . . . So this is what it's like to die . . . so soon, far too soon . . . so pointless. . . . Was this how that couple back there had felt . . . ?

Then for the second time Karen felt herself caught up short; spray flew as the water raced madly at her. Sam was gripping something; she tried to make it out through the rain that was slapping at her eyes . . . a rope . . . No, a hand . . . and then as the car drifted away, it swung in their direction. A final flash of its headlights showed it all. They'd formed a chain, the men, and the women, too . . . the women at the head, by the embankment. If Eve's strength failed, or Ruth's, then they'd be lost, all of them. . . .

But the line held, and slowly Karen fought her way forward. Finally the water was below her knees and she could walk. Gratefully, desperately, she rushed through the foaming water, Sam by her side, pulling her along; now Buddy at her other side, gripping her arm. A few steps more and they were free of the torrent.

Halfway up the embankment the seven of them huddled together, shouting at one another. Even shouting, they could barely hear; Karen had no idea who was saying what; everything was obscured by the furies attacking them.

"Can't go on. We'll have to go back!"

"Not to that house!"

"There's nothing else! We need to find shelter; too dangerous out here, too wet and too cold!"

Whoever had shouted it was, of course, correct.

They had no light. No one had thought to retrieve the flashlight from the glove compartment. Chilled and exhausted, they began to stumble forward.

Over and over they discovered they'd strayed off the road; found themselves tumbling down embankments, skidding on loose gravel. Karen didn't know if she could keep on; it was all chaos, all mad, frightening disorder. Twice she fell; pain shot through her knee, and she wondered if she was bleeding. In this hell of slashing rain and utter blackness there was no way to tell. She could be bleeding to death and there was no way she'd know it, no way she could separate the blood from the rain, no way anyone could know until, perhaps, it was too late. . . . Angrily she pushed the thought out of her mind. Nonsense. Have to go on. Don't distract yourself, don't weaken yourself.

She was near exhaustion when one of the men shouted, "There it is!"

A few steps more and she saw it, too; the lights of the house, glowing patches of sickly yellow-orange in a wilderness of black. Suddenly she realized the horror within the house had become meaningless; all she could picture was the light, the warmth, the shelter offered from wind and rain. She shook her head, half sickened by the thought. How easy, how terribly easy it becomes to ignore something—*anything*—if it serves to satisfy our needs, our desires. . . .

As they neared the house, their voices charged with relief, they began shouting and laughing. So they'd all been as desperate, perhaps even as frightened as me, Karen thought. Then she glanced up at Sam. He wasn't shouting; wasn't laughing. She peered into his eyes. Immediately she glanced away; wouldn't allow herself to look at him again.

This time their sense of relief on entering the house lasted scant seconds. Uncertainly, they huddled in the hall. "Home again, home again, jiggety-jig," Tim said sepulchrally. Ruth snorted her disgust, and then found herself shivering.

Sam noticed. "The living room would probably be best," he said. "Then maybe we can find ourselves some dry clothes."

Eve and Karen, as they followed him, glanced at each other. "Blankets might be better," Karen said. "Less . . . personal." Eve nodded gratefully.

Ruth looked irritable. "I'd prefer clothes myself," she said. "I assume you gentlemen feel the same." They all nodded.

"Okay," Sam told them. "I'll go up and see what I can find. Clothes *and* blankets," he said, glancing at Karen.

"I'll go with you," Tim volunteered. Sam nodded.

"I'm going, too," Ruth said.

"No!" Sam's voice was so sharp, their nerves so raw, they all started.

Like the others, Ruth had jumped, but she was hardly dissuaded. "I'm going, *too*," she said again, her voice dangerous. She'd be damned if she'd let them treat her like this, like a . . . *woman*.

If, as his expression suggested, he had been about to deny her again, Sam suddenly changed his mind. He shrugged. "All right, let's go," and he was on his way.

Ruth surveyed the house as they moved back into the hall and then up the stairs. Under any other circumstances, basically charming, she thought grimly. Victorians were all the rage these days; half her friends seemed to be restoring them or thinking of doing so. But now, despite all the lights, despite being here with friends, there was the suggestion of gargoyles, the sense of lurking terrors. Was it more than what she'd seen lying in the kitchen? Her sharp eyes swept the walls and ceilings; there were odd angles to this house; even the staircase, with all its twists and turns, seemed to be crazily skewed in some way she couldn't quite put her finger on. . . .

"Easy to get lost in this baby," Tim muttered, his fingers brushing uneasily across his lips. They'd paused on a half-landing. There was a small door on one side, a narrow passageway on the other. Sam swung the door open. The room looked tiny, like a storeroom. No clothes there.

After a quick glance down the passageway he led them on up the stairs to the second floor. A jumble of rooms opened off each side of the landing; there must be at least eight, Ruth found herself thinking, maybe even more. Rooms leading to rooms . . . and those rooms in turn leading to other rooms . . . leading to . . . She shook her head, impatient with herself. She was an adult, not a child. Ridiculous to be standing here, deliberately frightening herself.

"Look, a back staircase, too," Tim pointed out, then indicated the nearest room. "Why don't you guys check here while I take the next one down? Might save us some time."

She let Sam enter the small front room first. The rooms downstairs were cluttered and shadow-filled. This was a crabbed reflection; just as unpleasant in its own cramped way, just as full of dark corners and a sense of decay. Her eye was caught by a photograph on one of the dressers. She recognized the man and the woman; it couldn't have been taken that long ago. Standing between them was a girl in her late teens or early twenties. Pretty, in her way. Their daughter probably. Had *she* done it? She pushed the thought away, reached for the top drawer of the dresser . . . and found she couldn't make herself pull it out.

She stood there, her hands on the knobs, paralyzed, shamed by her reaction. There was a stir behind her, and gratefully she allowed it to distract her. Tim stood in the doorway, his face drained of color. He was pointing back toward the room he'd just left. He seemed unable to speak.

As Ruth rushed past him, Tim gasped, "Don't," but she wouldn't stop. Whatever it was, she had to face it, beat it. You couldn't let life get the better of you, not even once, because then it would *know* . . .

She and Sam reached the doorway at the same time. She looked in, and then, reacting instinctively, buried her face against his chest. Facedown on a narrow bed, a girl lay sprawled, her legs crazily bent, her long blond hair flung wildly on the blood-soaked quilt. The dim bedside lamp threw bizarre shadows over a face already twisted in terror and pain. The daughter. She'd been the last to die. There was no question of that. The hatchet was still buried in her flesh.

Slowly Sam pulled the door to. Ruth stared up at him, willing herself to be steady.

"We've got to change our clothes," he told her softly. "We'll all get sick if we don't. Tim can take you down, and I'll stay behind and find what we need."

She shook her head. "I'm all right. We'll do it together. And let's not say anything to the others when we go back down. It would be pointless to tell them, only unsettle them more."

Tim remained in the doorway, pulling himself together, while she and Sam rummaged. She yanked at the drawers, each one in turn, doing it quickly so there'd be no chance of what had occurred before happening again. *Will.* It was all a matter of will. She'd willed her life so far; had made it all work, all but the loneliness, and only lately had it occurred to her to try willing a change in that. She looked up at Sam and nodded to him. He returned her nod. They had enough now. All they had to do was go back to the rest of the group and get themselves dry. Simple, she told herself. It was all very simple; would be very, very simple from here on.

By the time she entered the living room she was sure she'd fully regained her composure. Then she saw the women's eyes flick wide open, and realized that the bright, unconcerned look she'd put on must have conveyed its own suggestion of gargoyles.

The horror obviously showed in Tim's and Sam's faces, too. Matt stared at them and then asked, "What is it? Is there more?" His question was very blunt, his voice very controlled, very normal. *Normal.* She seized on that and kept her eyes fixed on Matt, as if by doing so she could make everything all right again.

Tim said nothing. Sam tried to speak, but something seemed to catch in his throat. Finally, not looking at any of them, he nodded.

"How bad is it?" Buddy asked. "How many?"

"The daughter," Tim told him. "As bad as anything can be."

When Eve spoke, her voice was very sane, very practical. "We'll get dry first, change our clothes," she said, as if preparing a schedule for the day . . . breakfast, make sandwiches for the kids' lunchboxes. . . . "Then we'll take up the bodies and lay them out properly."

Tim shook his head. "We can't do that."

"Why not?"

"John Law," he told her. "The police. They have to investigate this whole thing. Dust for fingerprints, take bribes, whatever it is cops do. I mean, we're not exactly experts at this. If we moved the bodies, who knows what kind of evidence we'd destroy?"

What he said made sense. None of them had exactly been anxious to carry out Eve's suggestion anyway. Sam dropped what he was carrying onto the couch. "All right," he said, "we should have enough clothes and blankets here. There're towels, too. Dry yourselves down first."

Karen found a towel and a blanket and started to walk out of the room. Sam's voice stopped her short. "Where're you going?"

"To change."

"Do it in here," he told her emphatically.

"Why?" Karen asked, puzzled.

"Just a better idea," he said. Then, noticing the room had gone still, he looked around. Everyone was staring at him.

Ruth's voice was strident. "Why? *Why* is it a better idea?"

Sam shrugged. "*Easier* for you women to change in here. The four of us can stand with our backs to you."

Karen and Ruth exchanged glances. "You sound as if you're guarding us," Eve said, trying to make her voice sound light, and failing.

"Whatever you want to call it. Just change in here."

Karen and Ruth spoke almost at once.

"Wait a minute, Sam."

"We're not children. Tell us."

He shook his head. "No need," he said, glancing away from them.

Buddy cleared his throat. "The women are right, Sam. What's going on?"

Sam looked obdurate.

Ruth, her dark eyes flashing, charged in. "This is 1989, sweetie. We're all grown-ups, just in case you hadn't noticed the changes over the last few years, and that includes us women. If something's wrong, tell us. We're not going to go to pieces and start fainting and screaming on you."

"Speak for yourself," Tim said, forcing a grin. Then he added, "Yeah, come on, Sam. Spill it."

Sam's slender shoulders jerked. "All right," he said. "In the kitchen, and upstairs, too. The blood was still fresh."

For a moment no one seemed to understand. Then Eve asked, in a small voice, "You mean you think that when we arrived—the first time—it had only just happened?"

"Not too long before."

Buddy's voice was impatient, almost angry. "What makes you such an expert on blood?"

Sam shook his head. "Don't know any more than you do. Maybe less. But that's what it looked like to me."

Matt turned to Buddy. "He's right. It didn't register when I saw it, but he's right. Doesn't take that long for blood to thicken and turn color. It hadn't got like that when we saw it."

"You think whoever did it may still be here?" Ruth asked.

Sam's look was enough.

"Come on!" Buddy exploded edgily. "The guy's got to be long gone. He's not going to stick around here and let himself be caught."

Tim jerked his head in the direction of the storm. "*We're* here, aren't we? Even though we don't want to be?"

Buddy's mouth opened, as if he were about to continue his protest. But then he subsided. "All right." He shrugged and said quietly, "I suppose there's no sense in being foolhardy. We'll do it the way Sam said. Matt and I'll watch the hall."

4

As the three of them undressed, Eve furtively glanced at the other two women. Karen's body was just as she'd remembered it, slender, almost gaunt; big in the shoulders and with graceful, curving legs that made her seem far taller than she was. It was the kind of body that would hold up spectacularly over the years . . . at least from the outside, she told herself, her mouth twisting with the thought.

Her eyes swept over Ruth. Ruth's figure was a revelation. She'd become a real New Yorker. Must work out in one of those yuppie spas—she'd seen the ads—just about every day. Ruth had always had the bust, very full, very round; but now her arms and waist and thighs were even trimmer than when she'd been at school. Streamlined. Nothing like getting in shape, keeping your body healthy. Sometimes it worked.

Eve glanced down at her own soft body. The moisture she hadn't yet toweled off looked like dew. Morning-fresh, she told herself, tightly, fresh as a summer morning. There was a sudden slash of rain against the windows, and she quickly finished drying herself, then wrapped the blanket tightly around her. The other two women were done. "All right," she told the men.

They came in, found towels, and sorted through the clothing. Matt looked at the women: Ruth in an ill-fitting blouse and skirt, Karen and Eve draped in blankets. He wondered if Eve was nude under the blanket. She'd felt so soft in his lap, so yielding. . . . He held up a shirt and pants, tried another set, shrugged, and returned to the hall with them as Tim, from his station, called to the women: "Remember, if you peek, God'll strike you down. And if you peek at *me*, your esthetic sense will beat God out and do the job first."

Buddy waited for Matt to dress. "Guess I'll be in luck," he said as Matt drew on a rough work shirt and jeans. "Everything's a little big on you."

"Yeah," Matt agreed, unconcerned. "You should be able to dude yourself up just fine."

"How's the career going?" Buddy asked, toweling himself briskly. He'd been wet through longer than any of them, and his body was chilled. "The papers seem to have stopped following you."

"Not much to follow," Matt answered in his nonchalant way.

"No firsts?"

"Or seconds or thirds."

Buddy shook his head. The offhandedness of Matt's reply hadn't fooled him. He knew him well enough to figure how he must be feeling. Enough so that he didn't pursue the subject. "Heard one of your wife's records last week. Nice voice."

"Her manager says she's going to be a star," Matt responded, without any apparent emotion.

Buddy should have been feeling better. The rubdown had warmed him, and the clothes seemed to be fitting all right. Unfortunately, he observed to himself, a knack for empathy may do a hell of a lot for your friends, but it sure can dampen your own life. He was feeling Matt's pain. Both career and marriage going down the tubes, that's what it sounded like. Matt had been through two marriages before this. Not surprising if he blew the latest. Matt had never gone after women; there'd been no need to. They just seemed to gravitate to him, to demand he take them. Like Eve tonight. *Funny about that.* She'd never been the type before. He decided to ignore the implications of Matt's response. Not exactly the moment for a heart-to-heart. "Should be fun when the royalties start pouring in," he said. "Didn't you have a couple of kids?"

"By the first wife." Matt was rolling up his

sleeves, which were too long, although the fit around the neck was snug.

"See them often?"

"No."

Buddy glanced at Matt, who was leaning against the doorway. He looked as he always did, very relaxed. Relaxed about the kids he never saw, relaxed about his losing streak, relaxed about everything. . . . Except for his intelligence, Matt was so different from the rest of them. Except for his surprising intelligence—he'd been fifth in the class—he wouldn't have fitted in. "Guess this hasn't thrown you as much as the rest of us," Buddy said, a sweep of his hand indicating the kitchen and the room on the second floor. "I imagine you kind of get used to it. I mean, I suppose your life's in danger every time you race."

"I never think about death," Matt told him.

"Never?"

"What's the point?"

"You're right. No point. I think about it all the time," Buddy told him.

Sam and Tim were still dressing. "You've slimmed down some," Sam said as Tim did the best he could with the borrowed, far-too-large clothing.

"I'm a dude with an image to maintain. I mean, aesthete of the year, and all that."

"Heard you were a hotshot professor type now. What do you teach, anyway?"

"Hotshot *assistant* professor type," Tim corrected him amiably. "Religious history. Accent on medieval."

"Those thrilling days of yesteryear."

Tim grinned. "Thrilling's the word. You know how I spend my summers? Poking through manuscripts in dusty Italian libraries. Speed-reading in the original Latin."

"You serious?"

"About the speed-reading? No. My lips won't move that fast. But about the Latin, yes. You know why I learned it?"

"Tried to impress a girl?"

"Right. Figured I could seduce a nun or two. No, I learned it partly because of my profession. It's a good idea to find a niche for yourself. One with all sorts of twisting alleys, dark crannies, shadowy doorways. Medieval religion, going around spouting Latin. I mean, how many people know Latin today, even on a college campus? Who knows more than three things about the Middle Ages? So getting into an area like this, it's got to make you seem far smarter than you are."

Sam nodded, amused. "And the other part?" he asked.

"You listen when people talk, don't you? Almost un-American. Okay, the other part is strictly personal. Serious stuff. Sorry, but that's the way it is. See, I'm looking for an answer. I think it's back there somewhere, back in those manuscripts."

"God-type stuff?"

"God-type stuff." Tim nodded. "He exists. I'm

sure of that. *Existed,* anyway, which means he's got to still exist; we've just lost him somewhere. I walk into those unbearably hot libraries and I'm sweating like a pig as I untie those musty old boxes and pull out the manuscripts. All because I think—no, *believe*—there's an answer in there somewhere. You know, some kind of key. A key that will unlock it all and bring God back to us. Or to me, anyway." Tim grimaced. "How's that for pure egomaniacal insanity?"

"Seems to me you didn't used to think this way."

"Sure I did. At least I *think* I did. Just wouldn't admit it. Even to myself. Tried out everything I could think of first, as if that way I'd never have to get down to the nitty-gritty, could fool myself long enough. . . . Agnosticism, atheism, ashrams . . . from *A* to *A,* you name it, I tried it all. . . . But none of it worked. Or maybe it *did* work. Maybe it all led to where I am now." He stared at Sam, obviously uncomfortable. "What about you? Any grand organized stirrings?"

Sam smiled a little. "I've never been uncomfortable with the thought of being stuck here, all alone. No rhyme, no reason, no order."

They whirled as a loud cracking sound erupted. Somewhere a tree had snapped in two. "No order, eh?" Tim grinned faintly as they moved back into the living room. "You must be really stoked tonight."

Dry and warm again, the group's spirits had

lifted. There were remarks about dandies and making the best-dressed list, but eventually they fell silent. "God, what I wouldn't give for a cup of coffee," Ruth said.

After a murmur of assent from the group, Buddy volunteered. "I'll see what I can come up with."

"You wouldn't go in *there*?" Karen asked, alarmed.

"Hey, remember, I'm Golden Boy," Buddy said ironically. "Bad things don't happen to me."

"I'll go with you," Sam told him, rising.

"Never mind." Buddy shook his head. "Nothing's going to happen. And if it does—in the very unlikely event that it does—I can take care of myself. And in the just as unlikely event that anything happened in here, it'd be better if you stuck around, babe. Safety in numbers, and all of that." Without waiting for an answer, he left for the kitchen.

It was worse than Buddy had thought it would be. Far worse. He'd only had a brief glimpse before; had barely taken it in. The savagery was overwhelming. It had been demonic, maniacal . . . the hatchet had thudded into the bodies over and over again, twenty times, thirty times, more . . . long after there was need for further butchery. He turned toward the sink, afraid he was going to spill his insides. But the moment passed, and after a pause he began to move about the kitchen, keeping his eyes away from the floor.

The storm was far more intrusive in here; perhaps the walls were thinner. It was a step-down
kitchen, suggesting a room that had been tacked
onto the house. Or could this have been part of
the original house—it looked old enough—and
the rest added on to it? So many farmhouses grew
over the decades, room by room.

He found coffee in a canister. An electric pot
was standing near the sink, already plugged in. It
shouldn't take long. He opened a cabinet door
and found the cups. Atop the refrigerator was a
tray. He grabbed a paper towel and cleaned off
the film of grease. Good. He had everything. No
need to move around, less chance of accidentally
looking down . . .

He had no regrets at being in here. He'd
needed to be alone. Too many people, too many
things happening . . . Most of all, he needed to
be away from *Sam*. Wrong time for Sam to be
here, very wrong time.

A groan escaped him. Again he had the feeling
of compression, of suffocation. It was a feeling
that came more and more often these days. It
made no sense, just plain made no sense. He had
all the answers; did everything right; did it hon-
estly, too. It all should have worked.

"Chapter Eleven," Baker had suggested.

File for bankruptcy with a clause that allows
you to grab yourself a second chance. But he
hadn't given Baker a decision. Why should he file
that way? What kind of sense was there to it?

Over and over again he'd tried to make it work, so many times, so many different ways. . . .

It shamed him, but he couldn't help feeling grateful that the old man was dead. His father had passed the business on to him as if it were the beginning of a dynasty, something to be handed down over the generations. . . . He'd accepted it as such. But there was no new generation to pass it on to, and soon there would be no business. Soon there would be . . . nothing.

He stood there for some minutes, his head bowed. Then the coffee perked, and he started pouring it out. Done, he picked up the tray and started to return. *Sugar.* He'd forgotten the sugar. No doubt someone would want it. He looked around.

It was on the table. To get to it he'd have to step over the bodies. He shook his head. They'd have to do without. He picked up the tray, and again he stopped. No. Sugar's comforting for some. I'll have to do it. Very carefully he picked his way to the table. Then, as he reached it, he looked at the door to the next room. He decided to open it. . . .

Karen watched Buddy leave. She drew the blanket more securely around her and walked over to Sam, who was standing by the window. "Not getting any better, is it?" she asked, watching the storm-swept rain splatter against the glass.

He looked down at her. "My guess is, by now

this little rise is totally surrounded by water. We could be stuck here for a while."

"The seven of us—or the eight of us." She nodded. "You don't really think whoever did it . . . is still here?" She moved slightly, and felt her arm brush against his.

He shrugged. "I didn't try to stop Buddy from going back there alone. I guess that says something."

She was startled to find herself seizing on those words, clutching them gratefully. So she *had* been that uneasy. . . . She hadn't realized it till now. But of course . . . this awful night, that dreadful sight in the kitchen . . . then finding out there was more upstairs. She *should* have been frightened, she told herself. But now it was all right; would be all right. Sam had said what he'd said, and she was with him. She looked up. "Were you really in storms at sea? It sounds so romantic."

He smiled wryly. "I guess it was. Seemed romantic to me then. I was too young and too dumb to realize the kind of trouble we were in. The older men knew. You should have seen them. If I'd had any brains back then, I'd have figured all their praying and gibbering counted for something. I've never seen men more frightened."

"You were a passenger?"

The ancient window began to rattle violently, and he drew her away from it. "No such luck. A deckhand. On tramp steamers. Hopped the first one right after I left town."

"You still do it to me," she told him, shaking her head. "You still make me feel so ignorant, so sheltered. I've hardly left the state, while you . . ."

"I remember," he said. "All those questions you used to ask about New York. . . . Remember how afraid you were about my taking you there that first time?"

She laughed softly, nodding. "You seemed so magical, so sure. . . . Well," she said, her voice dropping, "you *were* magical." She glanced up at him. "I suppose you've been magical for a lot of women. Is there anyone now?"

"No."

"You haven't been married?"

He shook his head.

She shifted, and when she spoke she was surprised to hear how distant her voice sounded. It was as if he were someone she'd met at a party, someone who didn't interest her at all, someone she was being terribly polite to. "Were you at sea long?" she asked.

He didn't seem to notice. "Couple of years. That was my plan. You can save a lot when you're aboard a ship. At the end of two years I had enough to move to Mexico."

Mexico. "I remember now. We were going to live in Mexico. You were going to paint."

"You never believed me."

"No," she admitted, surprised she was admit-

ting it. "I was a small-town girl then. Things like
that didn't seem possible. Well, I'm still a small-
town girl. But now . . . now I think I'd believe
you. Is that where you live now, in Mexico?"

Almost as if angry, Sam shook his head and was
about to say something when he was interrupted.
Buddy had returned, carrying a tray filled with
cups and a large pot of coffee. "This should make
things cheerier," he told them as he set down the
tray.

"Even a trip to the morgue could make things
here cheerier," Tim said, then shrugged apolo-
getically as he saw the expressions on the wom-
en's faces.

Buddy was right. Although the house was
warm, drinking the coffee seemed to dispel a chill
all of them had felt. Their voices had become
lighter and more animated.

"The way things are," Eve said, "I don't suppose any of us is planning to sleep. What'll we do
to entertain ourselves?"

"No charades, nothing where we have to move
around," Karen said to Eve. "Not in our get-ups."
Like Eve she was bare beneath the blanket, had
been repelled at the thought of putting something so intimate as a dead woman's clothing next
to her skin.

"I hope we won't be subjected to any of those
tiresome word games," Ruth protested.

"That kind of puts an end to that." Tim
laughed. Then he snapped his fingers. "I've got

it!" His voice became ghoulish. "Let's put our heads together and figure out who did it."

"Who did it?" Matt asked. "You mean who . . ." He trailed off, as if reluctant to put it into words.

Tim didn't seem to notice. "That's right." He nodded enthusiastically. "There have to be clues. We can do the same kind of thing the fuzz will have to do. Probably better, considering the bimbos they have around here. Sure, we'll leave the scientific stuff to them; we can't touch anything." He tapped his head. "We'll stick to our noodles. Who knows? We could have the whole thing wrapped up by morning."

"That's a little sick, man," Matt told him. The others seemed to agree, and Tim shrank a little.

Sam, noticing, tried to ease the moment by suggesting— "Not much chance we'd have of figuring it out, anyway. Pretty unlikely there's any logic to it. That kind of thing, it'd have to be senseless, irrational, something done by a maniac."

Karen's voice was angry. "That sounds like you. Never any belief in order, in any real plan to life . . ." The words had leapt out unbidden. Embarrassed, she finished: "Not that I want to play Tim's little game anyway."

Ruth shook her head. With a thin smile, she said, "Tim was on the right track. All he had was the wrong crime."

As they turned toward her, they all became

aware again of the wind and rain assailing the house, the constant rattling of the windows, the unending banging of the shutters. . . . "What're you talking about?" Eve asked.

"What's happened here isn't what we should be getting caught up in," Ruth went on, her dark eyes shining. "What does it mean to us personally? Very little. While there's something else that does. *Should.*" She paused, and then asked, "Why do you think we're all here?"

Her question was met by blank stares. After a moment's wait, she tried it again. "Think of it. The seven of us, together. *Just* the seven of us. Why?"

"Why not?" Eve asked her lightly. "We were a group in high school. It's natural we'd have been drawn to each other tonight."

"That's just it." Ruth smiled triumphantly. "We *weren't* a group in high school. Only *once*. Only for one *night.*"

"You're crazy," Tim objected.

"Insane," Eve offered amiably. The three men seemed equally unconvinced.

But Karen shook her head. "I know what Ruth means," she told them. "At least I think I do. I mean, think about it. Sure, we *were* all mixed up together, one way or another. A set, I guess—the cream of the crop, and all that—but we never really hung out together, not all at once." She turned to Ruth. "Is that right?"

Ruth nodded. "Exactly. A set. Of which you

were the focus, Karen, you and Buddy. The two of you . . . well, of course you were involved with each other long before I came to town . . . from the first days of grade school, I know. I guess Eve may have been your friend even before Buddy. Then later you and I became friendly."

"That's right," Eve joined in. "And Tim was Buddy's friend even before grammar school. Then Buddy brought in Matt because they were both on the football and baseball teams."

"Okay, and when Sam came to town the two of us got friendly the first day he was in school," Tim contributed.

Eve nodded. "And of course Sam and Karen dated for a while when she and Buddy had the grumps. I guess Buddy via Karen is how you hooked up with Ruth, Matt."

Matt and Ruth stared at her.

"So we *were* all mixed up together," Eve finished. "But I see it now. Ruth's right. We *were* a set, led by Mister Perfect here"—she indicated Buddy—"but now that I think about it, it was a set that never came together. Not all together, not all in one place. Not till the night we graduated."

Karen turned to Ruth. "I still don't know what you're getting at," Karen told her. "What's all this got to do with Tim's bizarre suggestion?" She saw his expression and apologized. "Sorry. But you know what I mean. Under these circumstances . . ."

Ruth smiled smugly. "It's really quite simple. Why, for just the second time, did we come together tonight? I suggest it's because of guilt."

"Guilt," Karen repeated. She eyed Ruth curiously. "Before, you said that when we met at Raymond's funeral we all looked uncomfortable. Is there some kind of connection?"

"How quickly we're proceeding," Ruth said, nodding. "But that's to be expected, I suppose," she continued dryly, "considering the group I.Q."

"You're saying we could have saved Raymond," Eve prompted quietly.

"Am I?"

"Because we forgot him, and left him behind."

"I know why *I* was uncomfortable at the funeral," Karen said suddenly, almost violently.

They looked at her.

"Because I didn't come forward when they found Raymond's body. Because if I had, they'd have found out I was a criminal."

Matt looked puzzled. "Criminal?"

Karen's voice was self-mocking. "For breaking into the lodge."

Tim understood. "Yeah. Right. We were the good kids. We never did anything like that. Probably figured if we told anybody what we'd done, we'd go to prison." He shrugged. "Or at least get gossiped about, shame our parents. The joys of small-town living."

"I remember now. I think I started feeling

guilty from the minute Sam broke the lock," Eve said.

They all looked at Sam. Tim applauded sardonically. "I'd forgotten Sam was the master criminal. We got a little wild in that lodge, didn't we?"

"Compared to today's kids? Come on," Ruth scoffed. "We may have put away a bottle or two, smoked a few joints, broken a couple of chairs, but that was about it. No real damage. Not too many of us got our clothes mussed. If anyone."

"Wait a minute," Sam said. "Till tonight I didn't even know Raymond had committed suicide. Did it happen in the lodge?"

"In a shack close to it," Karen told him. "He hanged himself. No one knows why. No note, nothing."

Buddy shook his head. "I'm foggy about that night. When was the last time anybody saw him?"

"We started playing tag, I remember that," Karen said. "You know, like it was the last time we could ever act like kids. I'm pretty sure I tagged Raymond once. He was small, not that fast."

"We played hide-and-seek right after that," Eve told them. "Just inside the lodge. Everything else was out of bounds. I remember you saying that, Tim, after the first time we played it. Someone had hidden outside."

"Me," Matt admitted. "Funny, I hadn't thought about that night for all these years. But it's coming back to me now. You really got annoyed," he told Tim.

"I was big for rules in those days." Tim shrugged. "Okay, so does anyone remember catching Raymond when he hid out?"

"I think I did," Ruth said. "Maybe the first time. But we played more than once."

"All right. After that?" Sam asked.

They all looked at each other. "The cream of the class draws a blank," Tim said at length.

"Not surprising," Buddy told him. "It's been a long time. A long, long time. Fifteen years. We're all getting a little frayed around the edges." He shrugged. "I'll tell you what *I* don't remember. I don't remember why that little creep was with us that night." He looked at the others; searched their eyes. "How about the rest of you?"

Tim, looking puzzled, mused, "I never thought of that. Scum with cream. Unusual combination. What *was* he doing with us?"

"Another question, too," Sam said, when no one answered Tim. "Why did we leave without Raymond? Didn't we notice he was missing?"

"I'd say that's the more important reason for our looking uncomfortable at the funeral," Buddy told him glumly. "We must've had three or four cars with us. When we left that night I guess we all thought somebody else had Raymond with them. If we thought about Raymond at all."

"He was pretty easy to forget." Matt nodded.

Eve shook her head. "The kind you *wanted* to forget."

Ruth was about to interrupt when, without warning, all the lights went off.

There was general confusion, and then a tiny flicker of flame. Matt, the only one of them who still smoked, had lit a match.

Eve, caught up in the discussion, had almost forgotten where they were. Suddenly, the uneasiness that had been with her the whole evening was back. She attempted humor. "That's all we need, the electric lines going down. Well, it's an old farmhouse. Till the lights come back on, we can make do with candles. They've got to have some around here somewhere."

"I think all the lines were down before we got here." Sam shook his head. "Didn't you hear the humming from the cellar? Sounded like they had a generator going. Anyone here know how to fix one?"

Karen was fumbling along the top of the bookcase that stood against one wall. "Here's a candle!" she cried. Matt lit it, and by its flame they were able to find others. As the room became brighter, their voices, strident in the darkness, grew calmer.

"That's better," Tim said. "Not great, but better."

Matt took one of the candles. "I'll have a look at the generator," he said.

"I'll tag along with you," Tim told him. "Everyone needs a sidekick."

"As long as you're going to be down there," Ruth suggested, "if you can get the thing working, see if there's a clothes drier. It'd be nice if we could get back into our own clothes." Their clothing, still dripping, was draped over the dining-room chairs.

As the two men left, Ruth observed acerbically, "Not that it seems to matter. We've been pretty damn relaxed about taking these peoples' clothes and blankets, drinking their coffee, using up their candles, fiddling around with their generator. Fifteen years later, we don't seem to have lost our gift for ignoring the dead."

5

Tim's heart sank. "I knew it," he murmured as Matt swung the door open. "I knew we were going to have to go through this damned kitchen to get to the cellar."

As bad as it had been in full light, it was worse now. The flickering candlelight fluttered grotesquely over the two bodies. Despite himself, Tim found his eyes drawn to them. When he jerked his head away, he rasped, "Got a great thought. What if there're even more of them . . . down there?"

"Give us a pretty good story to scare our grandkids with," Matt suggested calmly as he opened a door and found it led only to a back kitchen or a shed of some kind. In the dim light he could see tools hanging on timbered walls.

"Right. If my heart holds out till then," Tim

answered in dismay as he realized he'd have to walk back past the bodies to get to the door at the other end of the kitchen. When he reached it, he glanced back at Matt, who was a few steps behind him. The sight reassured him. Like I'm with my goddam father, he told himself. Like I'm still ten years old. He opened the door, and was assailed by a strong musty odor. "This's got to be the cellar. One with a dirt floor. You can smell it."

The steps he descended were bare wood. Very old and very worn, they creaked resoundingly with each footfall. Tim's candle guttered. He stopped and cupped his hand around it, waiting till the flame was full again.

When he'd reached the bottom, Tim advanced a few steps, then stopped. He'd been right. The floor *was* dirt. He held the candle out to the side until its feeble light fell on a wall. It was stone, unpainted, apparently not even cemented. Almost like being in a grave, Tim found himself thinking. He felt oddly cut off, then realized why. Down here, he could barely hear the storm. "You notice how quiet it is down here?" he asked Matt, who grunted an affirmative. "I kind of miss the noise. Almost as if I've gotten used to the storm. Like it's comforting in some kind of crazy way," he continued, more to himself. He began to move the candle in an arc, stopped midway, and turned to Matt. "There's your baby," he said. Together they advanced on the furnace and the small electrical generator beside it.

He held the candle up as Matt bent down to look things over. "Could you move off a little?" Matt asked after a moment. "You're kind of in my way." He'd set his own candle on the generator.

"Story of my life," Tim murmured. He sighed and began to inspect the rest of the cellar. The more he looked, the more enormous he realized it was. He held the candle high. Christ, he told himself, it seems to stretch into eternity. Its dankness had depressed him from the beginning; the endless, looming shadows only made it worse. But he forced himself farther into the gloom, peering into the crates that were scattered haphazardly over the earth floor, investigating a small closet and two wooded-off areas that had once held coal. There were still a few lumps, dust-covered, left in the bins. There was a faint snapping noise, and he turned.

Matt was on his feet. "Nothing I can do with this," he said.

"What's wrong?"

"Somebody screwed up the armature."

Tim nodded. No big problem. They had candles; it wasn't cold enough to need the furnace. They could get along without the generator. He headed toward the stairs. Then something struck him and he turned back to Matt. "How do you mean, somebody screwed it up? You mean, somebody did something to the generator where after a while it just wouldn't work anymore?"

Matt shook his head. "Not exactly. Happened all at once."

Blood was beginning to buzz through Tim's head. "Wait a minute. I don't know anything about motors. Tell me so I understand."

"Somebody screwed up the armature. Messed it up," Matt repeated, his voice unemotional.

"When?" Tim asked. He was annoyed now. "Last month? Last week? *When?"*

"Had to be tonight," Matt said.

"Tonight. Like maybe two hours ago?"

"No. Just now. When the lights went out."

"You mean someone screwed up the armature and right away the lights went off? All the lights."

"That's right."

"We were all together in the same room."

"I know."

"Don't try to jive me, man," Tim cried, growing agitated. "As it is, I don't want to have to step over those two bodies again. And to do it knowing that whoever butchered them is still in this house . . ."

"Afraid you're not going to have much choice," Matt told him. He showed no signs of urgency, seemingly content to stand there and casually answer all Tim's questions.

"You always *have* been an easygoing son of a bitch," Tim burst out, anger mixing with fear. "Don't you know we're supposed to be acting like *cowards* right now?"

Matt looked at him calmly, saying nothing. Exasperation almost pushing out the fear, Tim began climbing the stairs. Then, halfway up, he turned to Matt. "Maybe *you* did it," he said. "I mean, when you were over there, I did hear something snap."

Matt shook his head. "Wish I had broken it. But that was just the tag end of it. It was hanging by a thread."

6

The slightly festive air that had filled the living room during the last half hour evaporated midway through Matt's report. Whatever fear there was, was concealed, controlled, but their faces had all become very serious, even grim. "You're sure there was no one else in the cellar when you were down there?" Buddy asked.

"I took a pretty good look. It's a mother of a cellar and it was dark, but I don't think I'd have missed him if he was."

"Okay. We can't just sit here. We'll go half crazy just sitting around *waiting*. Because if there is someone in this house, and he did sabotage that generator, he did it for a purpose. So we'd better find him before he finds us. Or satisfy ourselves that somehow Matt's wrong; that in some crazy way the machine just tore itself up."

"You mean search the house." Sam nodded.

"*Why?*" Karen's voice was plaintive, unbelieving.

Buddy stared at her.

"What's the point of looking for trouble?" she pressed. "All we have to do is stay here. There're seven of us. Whoever did that would never attack us."

"Whoever did *that* would never attack us?" Buddy asked, the implication of his question clear.

"All right. Maybe, if he's totally deranged. . . . But here we'd be safer. He'd have to come at us."

"It's late. Sure, we're all wide-awake now, but we've had a long day. What if we fall asleep?"

Karen shook her head in exasperation. "We'll post guards."

The corner of Buddy's mouth jerked into the semblance of a smile. "Trust people who're just as tired as us to stay awake? Sorry, kid, I don't have the faith in my fellow man you obviously have."

"I think Buddy's right," Sam said. "I know I'd feel a whole lot better if I got an answer one way or another."

"Right. You and I could go through the house."

Ruth shook her head vehemently. "While Matt and Tim protect us helpless womenfolk? Nothing doing. I agree we should search. But what I say is, it'd be safer if we all did it together."

"That'd make for an awful lot of clumping around," Buddy told her.

"Give all sorts of notice," Sam agreed.

"Seven can be as quiet as two." Ruth dismissed them. "Who's going to hear anything with all that racket going on outside, anyway?" She looked at Eve. "Don't you think?"

"I've been to too many drive-in movies," Eve answered wryly. "The woman stays where it's safe and then spends the rest of the scene hitting high C. I'm going along. You will, too, won't you, Karen?"

Karen nodded.

Buddy shrugged. "The New Women. Okay, but that double staircase gives our man—or woman," he added sarcastically, "too much opportunity to split if he hears us coming. I think we'd better take it from two sides at once. Any of you women *New* enough to want to go through the kitchen to get to the stairs? Otherwise, Matt and I can handle it, and we'll all meet up on the second floor."

"I'll go with you," Ruth said, her stare a challenge.

Buddy didn't bother meeting it. "I'll say this about you," he told her. "You haven't changed a whole lot in fifteen years." He lifted the poker from the fireplace and told Tim and Sam, "One of you take this. Matt and I can rummage around for something for ourselves in the back kitchen."

As the three left, Karen turned to Eve. "We'd better change. We can't move around much in these blankets." Quickly the two women began to draw clothes on under the blankets.

Entering the kitchen, Ruth felt herself falter. She'd only gotten a glimpse before; hadn't seen till now just how very, very bad it was. Steeling herself, she followed the men to the back kitchen. There Buddy removed a pitchfork from the rough-hewn wooden wall; Matt selected a pick. There was a small sickle on the wall near her. With a shrug she took it off the nails it hung on. She couldn't picture herself using it, but perhaps it could serve as a deterrent . . . if there *was* someone.

If only this damned wind and rain would stop, she told herself as they moved through the kitchen to the back stairway. *That's what's really bothering me. Hell on the nerves, all this constant roar and whine. Be much better otherwise. Far better. Probably nothing going on anyway. All this because of Matt's paranoia. Men with their macho machine diagnoses* . . . More than once she'd caught a man pontificating about the innards of a motor when all along it was obvious he knew nothing. True, Matt had spent his life around cars, but still, he was a race-car driver, not a mechanic. . . . She cursed to herself as she felt her heart pound against her ribcage.

We're doing the kind of thing grown-ups do, Karen told herself humorously as she carefully followed Sam up the stairs. *Acting like we'd expect grown-ups to act if all of this were real. But of course it's not. It's absurd. Things like this don't happen in real life.* Then she remembered the bodies. *All right,* she told herself fiercely, *but to* other people. *Not to me, not to the rest of us. Granted, anything is possible, but what are the odds? Astronomical, certainly, against anything happening here, to any of us. Too many of us.* And how likely was it the murderer was still here? Long odds, and even longer that the seven of them would mean anything to him. Of course, all odds flew out the window if there was no logic to any of this . . . if Sam was right, that this was the product of chaos . . . Damn Sam. *Damn* him.

He'd always had this quality. This ability to unsettle her with the things he said, the things he did. Now he'd done it again. His certainty that there was no logic to any of this had come back to her, shaken her. Without logic, everything was madness. With madness there were no rules, not even any odds to give comfort, to let you know you had a chance. She looked behind her at Eve and then at Tim, who was bringing up the rear. She produced a smile for them. When her eyes swung forward, she kept them on the stairs, away from Sam.

They'd searched all the rooms on the first floor and found nothing. Now Sam had paused on a tiny landing. He swung his candle and she could see the half-hidden outlines of a small door. He turned and motioned, then pulled the door open. The others followed him into the room. There was barely space for them. It was a storeroom of some sort, jammed with odd pieces of furniture, uncovered boxes, ancient storm windows. An old, very bad oil painting stood up against a wall. . . . That was all. The floors were bare, the wood very old, very neglected. There was a narrow closet in one of the far corners. Carefully Sam pulled at its door, then stood back and let it swing open. After a pause he looked cautiously inside. Nothing. He turned and shrugged at them, then nodded for them to leave.

Once outside, they started down a small passageway that stood opposite the small room, but it became quickly apparent that it was a blind alley.

Karen glanced behind her again as they started back up the stairs. This time Eve and Tim looked more relaxed, reflecting her own feeling. So far, nothing. Of course, at any moment . . . But still, so far, nothing. Ruth seemed to have been right; the four of them weren't making any more noise than one or two might have. What few small sounds they did make blended in with the howling going on outside. There was no way anyone would be alerted so long as they remained this quiet.

They reached the top of the stairs, and Karen realized exactly how right Ruth had been. The others were just coming up the back staircase. They seemed to be making no noise at all. She smiled thinly. Buddy had led the way. Then Ruth, with Matt behind her, sandwiched between two men, just as she and Eve had been. She and Eve hadn't objected; she doubted that even Ruth had. A chink in the armor of the New Woman, or simply an acknowledgment of superior upper body strength? She glanced back at Tim, who was shorter than any of them, weaker.

The two groups joined, and slowly, room by room, they began exploring the second floor. Ruth found she'd been right again; rooms did lead into other rooms. They kept finding themselves turned around, lost, unsure of where they'd been and where to go next. Eve began to giggle, but a severe look from Ruth stopped her.

They left the room where they'd found the girl for last. Only Buddy and Sam entered. When the two came out, shutting the door behind them, they all breathed easier.

Only the attic was left. As they mounted the stairs, the attic's heavy, faintly woody aroma brought back memories; memories of their own attics or the attics of friends; rainy afternoons spent playing in them or searching old boxes and trunks for treasures. But even then there had been something unsettling about the smell, and now as they climbed it was even more so. Here the storm was almost palpable; the rain burst like buckshot against the shingles, which shuddered from the attack and the ceaseless winds that tore at them.

The attic was huge, hangarlike, all one great

vaulted area. As they crowded together at the top of the stairs, they saw the flooring was hit-or-miss; spaces yawned open, dirty-looking cotton insulation half filling the gaps. The drafts up here made the candles gutter continually; even without that interference there would have been far from enough light. Dark shapes loomed in the blackness.

They looked at each other and then began to move forward, the men ahead of the women now; all of them slowly, quietly investigating: furniture, trunks, crates, jumbled piles of flotsam. The going was slow and they kept darting looks behind them, aware that anything rushing toward them could hardly be heard.

When they reached the far end of the gloom, Buddy spoke. "I guess that's it. Whoever was here seems to be gone." The casual tone of his voice, the first voice they'd heard in some minutes, evoked a sense of relief that flooded through the group so intensely, it felt almost like pleasure.

They laughed and joked as they came down the stairs, Tim deliberately making thumping noises with his feet. Again Karen found herself thinking of the dead so near them, but it couldn't be helped. Life did go on, and God knew they needed to break the tension somehow.

"It's over, isn't it?" Karen sighed as they entered the living room. "It's over and we don't have to worry anymore. The generator broke down all by itself."

"Right." Tim seconded her. "That generator could have torn itself up all on its own. I don't care what Matt says. In this life, anything's possible."

"Anything's possible," Karen repeated, almost dreamily. *"Anything.* For instance," she went on, her voice strangely hollow, "here we are, worrying about our suddenly having what happened to *them*"—she waved her hand in the direction of the dead—"happen to *us*. But what if it's really the other way around?"

They regarded her blankly. "What do you mean?" Eve asked.

"What if this isn't a hurricane after all?"

"One hell of a sun shower, if that's the case." Tim shrugged.

Karen ignored him. "I mean, what if it's a storm created by a nuclear explosion? One that's wiped out the rest of the world. Everyone *but* us."

"Hate to be your kids when you tell them a bedtime story," Tim tried again. He found himself looking at Buddy and Matt for approval. Buddy gave him a small grin.

Karen shook her head impatiently. "Haven't the rest of you ever had the same thought? Woken on a gray, gray morning when there's no life in the sky, and no sound at all from outside? I remember more than once when I was a little girl, waking up like that and thinking about being the only one left in the world. That the bomb had destroyed everything, everyone but me."

Ruth shook her head, suddenly sympathetic, in the first sign of softness she'd shown all night. "How terrified you must have been," she said, "at that age to feel yourself prey to chaos."

"Chaos?" Karen felt oddly shaken. She'd never thought of it that way. "That's Sam's word, not mine."

Buddy regarded Sam with amusement. "Never knew that about you, Sammy. So chaos is your bag?"

Sam shrugged, his lean face half hidden in shadow. "Guess so. I do believe there are no rules," he said quietly. "Even the so-called rules of the universe are rules only because we've made them that, forced them into being rules. The way you might force the wrong piece into a jigsaw puzzle to fool yourself into thinking you've completed it. There are no real rules except for the ones people make. To survive, we have to follow the best of those rules. But some of us can't. So even there it's all chaos, sooner or later."

"Chaos," Eve murmured. "Then perhaps chaos is the greatest rule of all—it would explain so many things . . . perhaps everything."

"I don't agree," Tim broke in. "I think there's a reason for everything. If there ever really was some kind of disaster, and we wound up the only ones left . . . then there'd be a reason behind our surviving. Good or bad, there'd be a reason."

"*Good.* The reason would have to be *good*," Karen said fervently.

"Why's that?" Buddy asked, cocking an eyebrow.

She glanced at the group. "Well, look at us. We're all bright people, decent people. Sam says there are no rules except for the ones people make. Some people can't follow those rules, Sam says. But *we* could. So we'd have a chance to start a whole new world, a world the way it always should have been. A world that this time would work."

Ruth laughed. "It doesn't happen that way. Yes," she agreed, "we are some kind of an elite. From every indication, we're far better people than most, more honest, more ethical, more rational. But that's on the surface. That's when there's no real strain. What would we be like when the veneer came off?"

"*Veneer?* Come on." Tim sneered. "*What* veneer? In a town this small? We all grew up knowing each other's business. Who here except Sam had the remotest *shot* at acquiring veneer?"

"That's pretty naive, even for an academic type," Ruth scoffed. "I imagine we shouldn't have to delve too deeply to find out a few new facts about you. Intriguing facts, in their sordid way." She smiled wryly as Tim suddenly looked uncomfortable.

"Then you're saying we're no better than—than the *thing* who murdered those poor people," Karen protested, disturbed by the direction the conversation had taken.

"For the moment, of course we're better," Ruth snapped. "But only for the moment. Who knows what might surface under the proper circumstances—maybe even before this night is over." Her eyes took them all in. "And of course if Karen's childhood fantasy did come true—if we *were* the only people left in the world—think of what could happen then. Undoubtedly *would* happen. Four men. Only three women."

"I like the odds," Eve broke in, her blue eyes mischievous. "Think of the fun we'd have, Ruth, three men fighting over the two of us."

"Three? Over just the two of us? Why?" Ruth responded dryly.

"Well, Karen's spoken for. So she'd be out of it."

"You think so? I'm not so sure," Ruth drawled, her eye falling slyly, tauntingly, on Sam. Then, during the uncomfortable silence that followed, she said, "I'm afraid this damned storm and everything that's gone with it has given me a tremendous headache. Does anyone have aspirin?"

No one did. She stood and murmured, "I'll look in the bathroom. There's probably something up there."

Buddy rose. "I'll go with you."

Impatiently she shook him off. "I decided not to say anything when we went up the stairs, but believe me, I've felt protected enough to last me through the evening, if not for a lifetime. I'll be all right."

"You shouldn't go alone," someone said. "Just in case . . ."

"*Watch* me," she answered. As she neared the hall, she turned. "You realize, of course, that all this about the bomb—it's been our way of evading the subject." When she saw the lack of comprehension on their faces she went on, "The subject of Raymond's murder."

A high, startled laugh broke out of Tim. The others seemed bewildered.

"I don't understand." Sam shook his head. "I thought we'd all agreed. It was a suicide."

"It *was*," Karen told him firmly. Matt, Tim, and Eve nodded.

Ruth shook her head. "No."

"That's what the police said," Eve protested. "That's what the newspaper said, the TV."

Ruth's smile was supercilious. "All those mysteries you used to read, Eve. Probably still do. It's obvious they haven't been of much practical help."

A look of annoyance crossed Buddy's face. Ruth was obviously toying with them, enjoying it. "What makes you think it was a murder?"

"I *know* it was a murder."

"Despite what the cops said."

"Yes."

"Why?"

"Something very obvious. Something that should have been very obvious to all of you."

"What?"

Ruth shook her head. "I need to find that aspirin. Think about it. All those state-of-the-art cerebrums. You're sure to hit on the answer. And if you don't, I'll tell you when I come down. Then we can go on to the next step." She turned, and left.

When no one followed her, she wasn't surprised. Long ago she'd learned to say no in a manner that brooked no opposition. As she neared the stairs, a breeze from somewhere plucked at her candle, and she stopped, cupped her hand around it, and waited for the flame to recover. It was so fragile, a speck in the darkness. And yet how much light it cast; David vanquishing Goliath.

Or at least keeping him at bay, she thought, peering beyond the candle's glow into a wall of black. She started up the stairs, moving slowly to ensure the candle's remaining lit. Nearly halfway up she paused again. There had been a sound of movement somewhere above her. A chill ran through her body. She shook herself angrily. *You're being like a child, a schoolgirl, all wide-eyed after some campfire tale of madness and terror.* Irritably, she resumed her climb.

Downstairs, Ruth's parting words hung over the group. They tried to puzzle it out but made no headway. "Ruth's always been a little odd."

Buddy shrugged. "It was probably just her idea of a great exit speech."

"Right." Tim nodded. "When she comes down and we ask her what it's all about, she'll claim she never said it."

"I don't agree," Eve demurred. "Ruth *is* a little odd, but not that odd."

Karen nodded. "I'm with Eve. Ruth wasn't putting us on. I'd bet on that."

Sam rose. "Afraid I can't be much help. I don't remember Raymond at all. What I do know is that I'm half starved. I'm going to take the cups back in, clean up a bit, and then forage for food. Anyone else like anything?"

Despite herself, Karen nodded. She was painfully hungry. There was something obscene about it; in the midst of all this horror, life went on. Nerves began to cry out for caffeine, digestive juices began to stir. "I could get the fire going," she told him. "In case there's something you want to cook. We might be able to manage it over a fire. In any case, it'll give us more light." She wanted to offer to help him clean up, but she couldn't face what was in the kitchen. As he left she crouched in front of the fireplace. There were small logs to the side of it, and carefully, methodically, one after the other, she began arranging them across the blackened andirons. There was a rustle, and looking to her right she found Buddy crouched beside her. "I have something to tell you," he said, his voice hushed and urgent.

She stopped in mid-motion. Was it the light, or did he really look so terribly tortured? She'd never seen him like this. Suddenly everything that had always seemed so stable in her life began to teeter. With a little nod of her head she signaled him to go on.

"I'm going to lose the business."

The sounds of the shrieking wind, the clattering of the shutters, the explosions of the rain against the trembling windows, intruded on her consciousness again. "I don't understand," she said, her voice barely audible.

"I hoped I'd never have to tell you. Hoped I'd never have to tell anyone. I'm so ashamed," he murmured, his eyes not meeting hers. "Captain of the football team, valedictorian, most popular . . . I was supposed to succeed. I believed it, too. Why not? Success was all I knew." He looked at her, and she knew it wasn't the light. There was agony in his eyes. "But from the beginning . . . no matter what I tried . . . it didn't work. I didn't know why. I still don't know why."

Karen shook her head as if to clear it. "But the house . . . the cars . . . the way we live . . ."

"The savings went first. Then what my father had left us. After that, the loans began. Each time I thought that, somehow, I'd turn it all around. I never told you because I didn't want to worry you." He clenched his eyes shut and shook his head. "No. That wasn't it. I was too ashamed. So ashamed, I didn't go to any of the banks in town.

Didn't want the word to get around. I couldn't face failing."

She reached for one of the newspapers stacked near the wood and began to separate the pages. One by one she crumpled the sheets and tucked them underneath the logs. She did it very, very neatly, giving it every last bit of her concentration.

7

Ruth popped the two aspirin into her mouth and turned on the cold-water tap. She pressed her hands together, cupping them tightly, with just a small hole showing at the top, then held them beneath the stream. She waited till the hollow between her palms was filled, then raised her hands to her lips, and swallowed the aspirin with the water. Funny. Her mother had taught her to drink that way when she was four, and she was still grateful to her for it. Particularly tonight, when she'd found she couldn't bring herself to use the glass that stood on the sink.

Halfway through drying her hands, she paused and stared at the bathroom door. She wished now she hadn't closed it behind her. Habit, of course. Damned habit. A sudden rattle of the window-pane startled her, and she swore under her breath.

She had to admit it now. That little noise on the landing had unnerved her. She found herself wondering how Sam, if he were in this situation, would be reacting. Reluctantly she found herself deciding he'd simply turn the knob and walk out, shrugging off any thoughts of what might be lurking outside that closed door. Damn men. Always so confident. So much more confident than most of them had a right to be. Not true of Sam, of course. In his way, he had as much going for him as Buddy and Matt.

Impatiently she finished drying her hands, seized the candle, and turned toward the door, then found she had to wait as the swift movement of her hand nearly extinguished the flame. The wind was so fierce now that the door had begun to rattle. When the fragile wisp of light reasserted itself, she started to turn the door handle. And stopped.

Fear was flooding through her, smashing at her last defenses. She was terrified. It was too plain now not to admit it. She was as terrified as if she were a little girl. Someone *had* destroyed the generator; had done it while they were in the house. And like a fool, she'd shown off; insisted on coming up here alone, sick of Buddy's gallant ways. No, furious. Because it had been Buddy who'd volunteered, not Sam.

Sam. She found herself thinking of him now as if he were her only hope. If he were here, she'd be all right. He'd put his arms around her, calm her fears, protect her. She pictured herself whimpering like a child, her head falling against his chest.

She'd come to the reunion because of Sam. Because he might be there. *Insane.* There'd never been anything between them. There'd never been a chance for anything to happen. Almost as soon as he'd moved here, Karen had established her claim to him. How envious Ruth had been. All along Karen had had Buddy, and then just as Buddy and Karen had split, Sam had arrived to take his place.

And yet she and Sam had had their moments together. That wonderful afternoon in the school's basement when they'd volunteered to put away books. Sam had been friendly, his look and voice had been kind. And yet . . . there'd also been the sense of danger, the danger she'd always responded to. Something about him, something unknown and dark . . . frightening.

Angrily she shook herself. Nothing like finding yourself to be a stereotype. The illogical woman. Here you are, frightened out of your wits, and in the next breath you're longing for a man whose strongest attraction for you is his danger. No wonder your life is what it is. You're an idiot. You don't deserve any better. She jerked the bathroom door open, pushed out into the darkness.

And then stopped. Had she heard something? Had something moved? She waited, listening, but the beating of her heart and the fear that roared through her drowned out everything else. She longed to moan, to cry out. Instead, with all the strength she had left she forced herself forward.

Up here the noise of the storm seemed to be worse than downstairs. Perhaps it was intensified by the height, the way New York's street noises became so much louder the higher up you went in a building. No, that made no sense. . . . But she tried to cling to the thought anyway. New York . . . a place so far removed from all this, the stark insanity of this storm, the thick black shadows that stretched out before her, alongside her . . . behind her.

She continued along the hall and then realized she was about to pass the room that held the girl's body, recognizing it by a small bookcase near the doorway. The door stood open. Odd. She thought she remembered Sam shutting it. An impulse seized her. It was a compulsion she couldn't fight. *She had to look.*

She raised the candle and watched as the light fell over the edge of the bed. The legs—legs of a young girl, life only just beginning. Had she ever had the chance to love, to hold a man close against her . . . ? She moved into the doorway, raising the candle so that the light passed slowly along the girl's body.

Her hands stopped, jerked back, then moved forward again, shaking. The light was dim, but there was no question. *Where was the hatchet?* It had been there before, but now it was gone!

She rocked back, then forced herself forward, advancing into the room. It *must* be here; had probably just torn free, fallen . . . Had Sam or Buddy removed it when they went into the room? She was certain she hadn't seen either of them stoop over the body. She tried to avoid the awful sight of the girl's one open, staring eye as she moved the candle around desperately. *Nothing.*

Maybe I'm wrong. Maybe I only thought I saw a hatchet that first, awful time. But I did see it. Maybe Sam or Buddy did remove it. I might have been distracted; looked away. But then where is it? Not here. They didn't come out with it. No, stop! Can't keep thinking like this. Find out when you get back downstairs. To the living room. To your friends. It'll be all right then. For now, just think that the men took it . . . did something with it.

She turned and began making her way down the hall, her heart near to bursting, one explosion after the other pounding against her breast. *Damn.* She had to pause. She'd been moving too quickly. Can't do that or the candle will go out. As she waited, sheets of rain were thrown so fiercely against the window that they sounded like hailstones.

Was that another sound now, immediately in front of her?

I can scream. I'll scream, and whatever is in front of me will run away. Or the others will race

*up the stairs, get here in time. That's it. I can
scream, and then everything will be all right.*

But she couldn't scream. Couldn't be that
much of a hysterical ninny; couldn't shame herself in front of all of them. *There's nothing out
there ahead of you, nothing out there but the
dark, and all the nameless fears the dark can call
up, if your nerves are bad enough.*

She moved forward another foot, two, and then
breathed a sigh of relief. She was near the stairs.
*This ordeal is almost over. Less than a minute
from now I'll be in the living room, secretly
laughing to myself, calmly waiting for the storm
to end. Even if it doesn't . . . just a few more
hours till dawn . . . the storm will be just a
storm then, nothing more. . . . And what if it's
the storm Karen wondered about, the nuclear
storm, and there were just the seven of us? Then
I'll fight Karen for Sam, dammit. Fight her and
win.*

There, she was feeling better. She reached the
head of the stairs and fumbled in the gloom for
the banister. She found it and started down, her
movements hesitant now, she assured herself,
only because of the need to keep the candle
alight.

One step down, two, three . . . She halted.
For these last few moments she'd been feeling
that something was wrong, was out of kilter. Now
she knew what it was. She'd taken the wrong
staircase. This damned house was so confusing;

had her turned all around. She was going down the backstairs, the ones that would lead her into the kitchen. She'd have to go into that room first, walk past those horrible, sprawled bodies. . . . She couldn't face any more of that. She'd have to turn back.

But then she found she couldn't.

She couldn't turn and face what was behind her. *There's nothing behind you,* she told herself fiercely, but it didn't matter. She couldn't do it. The fear was too great. There *had* been a hatchet. And none of the men had removed it. She could no longer fool herself about that.

Her eyes fell on the patterns the candlelight traced on the walls. They were bizarre, and erratic in movement. *Of course they're moving, you damned fool. Your hand is trembling. This is the most frightened you've ever been. Think of it as a first, as an experience. Someday, that's all you'll think of this as: an experience.* But then there was a dreadful crooning sound, and after a moment she realized it had escaped from her lips. She was close to fainting; fear was paralyzing her. She had to go on. *Now.* Before it was too late. Before she crumpled; fell into a swoon; tumbled down the stairs. There's your real danger, she told herself, and placed her foot out into space. She wanted to cry, to reach out for Sam, for anyone . . . for her mother. She set her foot on the step below, then stepped off with her other foot. And then she saw.

She wanted to scream, tried to scream, but nothing would come. The terror filled her; choked her; stopped up her lungs. . . . Coming toward her, coming toward her . . . There's no hope, none at all. She couldn't scream, couldn't move . . . *For God's sake, please, please . . . Mom . . . Mommmm . . .*

The scream rang through the house, chilling them. Instinctively, hearts racing, they sprang to their feet. While the shock of it kept the others rooted, Buddy reflexively ran in the direction of the stairs. Slowly, as if in a dream, the others began to follow. By the time they'd reached the hall, Buddy was already out of sight.

Eve found herself ahead of the rest. She'd seized a candle, but it had guttered out immediately; she was guided only by the sound of Buddy's footsteps. *Ruth.* Not *Ruth.* It was a mistake, some kind of awful mistake. Ruth had imagined something; lost her nerve; screamed.

Unable to see, she started up the stairs, stumbling forward in the dark, aware that behind her there was someone with a candle, but it was no help to her; it was too far behind. Her lungs were burning, her heart throbbing in great shuddering blows, but she kept going. She was using her hands on the stairs now, having lost the railing as she'd reached the little landing. As she neared the top of the stairs she could see a light ahead of her. Buddy must have done a better job than she at keeping his candle lit. Somewhere ahead of her there was a soft scraping noise, like the sound of a drawer closing.

She reached the second floor, then, her lungs flaming, staggered down the passage toward a light she saw ahead. "Buddy," she gasped, "Buddy!" Then she saw him . . . saw what he was crouched over.

Eve faltered, swayed, then caught herself before Buddy could leap to his feet and brace her. The terror that showed in her dead friend's face was somehow more terrible by far than all the other horrors of this nightmarish night. It was like the naked fright displayed by the corpse of a savagely assaulted five-year-old; so pitifully defenseless, so rendingly vulnerable, so heartbreakingly fear-stricken. Even the gaping, hideously scarlet wedgelike wounds seemed to exude the same vulnerability, the same sense of childhood innocence defiled. All of Ruth's longtime defenses fled, all the hardness vanished, all the bitterness dissipated . . . revealing so nakedly the lonely, lost child she'd still been somewhere deep inside. . . . Eve barely noticed when the others ran up, hardly heard their gasps.

Shaken, they all looked at each other. Then Karen noticed. "Sam!" Her hushed voice was frantic. "Where's Sam?" There were only the five of them on the stairs—the five of them and Ruth. They stirred uneasily.

And then turned, startled. Someone was running up the stairs toward them. Karen's hands jerked upward, instinctively protective. "Oh, God," she gasped. Then they saw it was Sam. He stopped just below Buddy, his eyes on what was left of Ruth. He appeared to be soaked through. "Thought I heard someone outside," he murmured, out of breath. "Brushing past the kitchen window. I ran out; couldn't find anything. On the way back in I heard . . . her . . . scream. Stumbled over those damned bodies when I ran for the stairs." Karen realized now why his hands were so dark. They were covered with blood. He must have fallen directly onto the bodies, his hands reaching down to stop the fall, blood rushing out, covering him. . . . She felt herself begin to sway, and reached for Tim as she found herself plunging into an unending black tunnel.

8

Karen opened her eyes. Of course. She'd been
sleeping, nothing more than that. Had drifted off
and dreamed it all, been racked by a nightmare.
Ruth was still alive; had never screamed. She remembered now. She and Buddy by the fire . . .
she turning away from him, unable to respond
. . . joining the others and their conversation.
. . . They'd been talking about Raymond, about
his death, about Ruth's odd certainty that it
hadn't been suicide. . . . That's what must have
caused the nightmare, all that talk about murder.
She must have dozed off, not realized she was
falling asleep. . . .

Still lying on the couch, she looked around.
There's Eve. And Buddy and Matt. Tim and Sam
. . . Ruth. Ruth must be somewhere near. . . .
Then her eyes dropped to Sam's hands. She

moaned. He'd obviously tried to clean them, but some of it remained . . . brownish red across his knuckles, a smear over a fingernail. Her moan became a sob.

Eve noticed. She rushed to Karen and knelt beside her, taking her hand. "It's all right. It's going to be all right," she told her.

But Karen knew it wasn't. And that it was far from over. The wrenching sounds of the storm assaulted her ears, and her eyes traced the macabre patterns cast on the walls and ceiling by the trembling flames that dotted the room. They were cut off, alone, trapped in a house with a madman.

"Insane," she told Eve feverishly. "He *has* to be insane. The others . . . There might have been some explanation . . . you know, an attempted burglary, maybe an argument . . . But Ruth . . . He had to be insane to do that."

Eve's expression was grave. "Probably," she said. "Probably you're right. But we'll be safe as long as we stay together. There are six of us. He'd have no chance. We'll be all right."

Karen nodded, not looking at her. As Eve had spoken, something had flooded through Karen that shamed her. A sudden feeling of gratitude that . . . if someone had to die, it had been Ruth who'd been unlucky, and not one of the men. . . . Four men still alive. Four men to protect her . . . Sickened, she shook her head. She couldn't allow the fear to bring her to this. She forced herself to a sitting position. She'd be all right. She'd *make* herself be all right. She looked at Eve. There were just the two of them now, two women. Eve's face seemed very pale and her lips were drawn tight. Their eyes met, and from her glance it seemed as if Eve understood; shared Karen's thought. Yes, just the two of them now. Two women, four men . . . Insanely, Karen found herself thinking, What if we *are* the only ones left in the world? She knew now Ruth had been right. Four men battling for two women. Would the savagery of it be any less frightening than this? *No.* She refused to believe it. They were good people, civilized people. They would make the world a better place. She rose, walked over to the fire, knelt, and very deliberately began feeding logs into the flames. Then stopped. There were only three logs left in the pile. She'd been profligate with the wood. When it all burned down, they'd have to search for more, go into one of the back rooms, or even outside. "I'm sorry," she said. Sam was standing beside her. He nodded. He'd understood.

A breath of hope stirred in her. "What time is it?" she asked.

"Still too long till dawn," he told her.

Karen's eyes were sharp as she glanced at him. Almost anyone else would have answered that differently, tried in some way to reassure her. Sam could have spared her, made his answer softer, or simply told her the time, skipped the allusion.

There had always been that side to him. Cruel, perhaps, sadistic. Or was it simply dispassionate? An equal to an equal; answering her as he would have answered one of the men. Damn. Why was she like this whenever she was with him? Always wondering, always uncertain, always . . . *drawn*.

Sam had turned toward the rest of the group. "Look," he told them, "the food I was gathering up just before . . . it's still sitting out on the kitchen counter. If anyone would like me to bring it in . . ."

Eve's fear, so far masked, broke through. "You wouldn't go back there alone?"

He shrugged. "Matt could come with me. Buddy and Tim could hold the fort here."

"All right," Eve said, her face lowered, ashamed of her hunger.

The weapons the men had carried during the search of the house were scattered throughout the room. Sam picked up the pitchfork and pick. Dried crusts of yellow mud fell off the pitchfork as he handed it to Matt. "In case we need an edge, this should give us one," he muttered. "Come on."

Tim watched the two men leave. His tones were wry as he said, "Odd. We professorial types don't seem to get many calls as enforcers."

Buddy was stationed by the door to the hall.

Tim had moved near the entrance to the dining room. Karen and Eve were alone on the couch. "I just realized," Karen said, searching for something normal, something comfortingly everyday, "I don't know what your children look like. Do you have pictures?"

With a grateful glance, Eve rummaged in her purse. Finding her wallet, she flipped through a few photo sleeves. Stopping at one, she handed the wallet to Karen. "Tommy is the eight-year-old. Jason's ten. The photo just before that is of Jim."

Karen looked at the children, then at the picture of Eve's husband. She'd met Jim at the wedding. He didn't seem much older, though he'd since lost most of his hair. The two boys could have been anyone's children. They resembled neither Eve nor her husband; looked the way most boys do when they're eight and ten years old, very nondescript, very much alike. A wave of feeling passed through her. "I envy you," she said. She deeply meant it.

Eve's eyes filled with tears, and Karen turned away. Foolish of me to say that. A man she loves, two children she loves, and now she doesn't know if she'll ever see them again; doesn't know if she'll live through this night.

After Eve had recovered, she asked Karen, "How about you? Not ready for kids yet?"

Karen's eyes fell. "We've tried to have them. Almost from the beginning. Ever since. We've been to all sorts of doctors. Nothing wrong with Buddy. Nothing wrong with me." She stared at the fire. "But I think maybe it has been me. I've been thinking that all evening. You know, that I'm fighting it somehow. Not because I don't want children. Because I don't want *Buddy's* children."

Eve looked shocked. "Why would you say that?"

"I don't know."

"I thought things were fine between you. You know, aside from the usual marriage things. I mean, you've always seemed to adore each other. From the second grade on."

"I suppose we did," Karen said slowly, not sure if even that was true. Had they ever really loved each other? It seemed so unlikely now. . . . "But . . . I don't know . . . it's as if suddenly I've seen that it's not working. That it never has. I mean, we were so young. Then we broke up. You know, in high school. After that, when we got back together . . . I think it was like a habit. A habit we couldn't break. A habit it didn't even occur to us we *could* break." She shook her head. "I'm not even sure . . . I mean, we went though life day by day, doing the things a husband and wife are supposed to do. It seemed like a marriage. But now . . . I don't think I ever wanted to have Buddy's children."

Eve's distress was genuine. "Maybe . . . maybe it's just because of all this, this . . ." She found herself unable to say it and continued, "Maybe it'll all change back to the way it was. I mean, the way it *really* was, not the way you're seeing it now . . . all change back to that when morning comes."

"Buddy told me something tonight," Karen said quietly. "I think he felt me slipping away, so he deliberately told me tonight. To keep me tied to him."

"Do you want to tell me about it?" Eve asked softly.

Karen stared at her. "I can't," she said finally, "for Buddy's sake."

The two fell silent, then looked up, grateful for the distraction, as Sam and Matt entered. They were carrying trays laden with food and drink. Quickly Buddy pushed a low table near the fire, and they all seated themselves on the floor around it, the men placed so that they could watch the entrances to the room.

Everything had been brought in one trip; neither man had any intention of returning to the kitchen. The table was piled high with food. There was white and rye bread, cheddar cheese, Swiss cheese, ham, salami, tuna fish, olives, crackers, molasses cookies, two half gallons of milk, and a half gallon of orange juice.

Their hunger was strong, and there was little conversation as they heaped the food onto their plates, pressed pieces of meat between slices of bread, poured milk and juice into earthenware mugs. Then, as they began to eat, conversation stopped entirely. But as the edge of their hunger dulled, talk slowly resumed. The food was commented on, small jokes were made.

Eve leaned back against the sofa. "I wonder why Ruth was so sure Raymond had been murdered?"

"What I'd still like to know," Tim murmured, "is why Raymond was with us. Was any one of us actually friendly with him?"

"I've been sitting here all night trying to get a fix on the guy," Sam said. He was sitting with his back to the fireplace, his eyes on the hall.

"You're lucky," Eve told him. "I remember Raymond too well. He was a repellent, loathsome, scrawny little toad."

"Sounds like you were ready to string him up yourself," Tim said dryly.

Eve looked as if she'd been struck.

"I remember he sat across from me in homeroom," Karen put in quickly, to break the tension. "I think around junior year. An undersized, skinny kid with thin, patchy hair—you know, with skin showing through around the sides of his head. He had a bad complexion, too; his flesh was almost gray, except where the blemishes were. And every time you caught him looking at you, he'd smile at you, a dirty kind of smile, as if he knew something nasty about you."

"The way creeps do," Eve said.

"The way creeps do," Tim agreed, as if anxious to make amends.

"I felt sorry for him," Buddy said simply.

"Yes. You would have." Karen nodded coldly. "You and Eve were always the bleeding hearts." Then she felt a flush of shame. "No, that's not fair," she hurried on. "You were the two kindest people in the class."

"I wasn't as kind as Buddy," Eve said grimly. "I couldn't make myseif feel sorry for Raymond."

"He was general courses, we were on the college track," Tim remembered. "That's why he's so hard to get a fix on. Mostly, I just remember him from gym. Always standing around with a weird grin, like he knew something the rest of us didn't. Wore grubby-looking shorts and T-shirts. His right hand was always sort of crooked up at his chest."

"Now I remember who you're talking about," Matt jumped in. "All night I've been racking my brains. . . . He was the little guy I gave a ride on my motorcycle. You know, the time I skidded on the gravel. He flew off. Only accident I ever had."

"Okay." Sam nodded. "I can see him now. Finally. You're right. He was like you all said." Turning to Matt, he asked, "Broke his legs or something, didn't he, when he went off the bike?"

"Hand," Matt said. "One of his hands got tore up pretty good."

"My God."

There was something in Eve's tone that made

them turn to her, something final about it, something . . . unsettling.

"My God," Eve repeated. "Ruth *was* right. It *had* to be murder. Raymond couldn't possibly have committed suicide."

"What do you mean?" Buddy asked.

"Think back to that night," Eve quavered, shaken.

"Okay," he said gently, going along with her. "We graduated. Got out . . . I don't know when. I think maybe we went home first and changed. Anyway, that was earlier in the day. That night we went out to the Falstaff Inn. The whole class. Danced, drank—ate, too, I guess. Maybe smoked the odd joint. Then the seven of us—I mean the eight of us—Raymond had to have been with us— the eight of us piled into our cars and drove off to that lodge, wherever it was. Somewhere in the woods outside Holtsdale. We broke in. Boozed it up. Told dirty stories. Drank. Horsed around. Left."

"What about Raymond?" Eve asked.

"What about him?"

"What did he look like?"

"Look like?" Buddy asked, puzzled. "Hey, I'm not Sam. I've remembered what he looked like all along. As clear as if it were yesterday."

"I don't mean that," Eve said impatiently. "I mean, what did he look like *that night*?"

Buddy shook his head and turned to Tim, who seemed to have an odd expression on his face.

Tim shrugged. "You got me. Pustulated, I guess."

Eve turned to the others. They stared at her blankly. "Remember? Two weeks before that night, Raymond fell off Matt's motorcycle."

Karen shook her head, unable to see what Eve was getting at. "I don't know. Was his hand in a cast?"

Eve's voice was very quiet, very intense. "Yes."

"Is that what you're getting at? That his hand was in a cast?" Buddy asked, as bewildered as the rest of them by Eve's agitation.

"Exactly."

"What difference would that make?" Sam shrugged.

"Remember Mr. Broughton? The biology teacher we had—for only part of a term? He was there one day and gone the next?"

Only Tim seemed to remember. "Yeah, vaguely," he said. "Jeez, I'd forgotten all about him. We *are* getting old, aren't we?" he said to the others. Then, turning to Eve, he continued, "What about him?"

"One day, after class, I made a remark about Raymond. Mr. Broughton said I should be kinder, that Raymond was a cripple."

"You mean emotionally," Tim prodded.

"No."

"Come on, I was in gym with him. He was no great athlete, but he was no cripple."

"That's what I thought, too. But after Mr.

Broughton told me, I watched him. Raymond was very clever about it. But I watched him and I watched him, and finally I knew Mr. Broughton had been telling the truth."

"Which was?" Buddy asked, a disbelieving smile on his face.

"Raymond couldn't use his left hand. It looked okay. Maybe a little skinnier than his other hand, but not that much."

"His left hand was useless?" Karen asked.

"Totally."

Karen was beginning to understand. "And which hand did he break?"

"His right."

Karen stared at Eve. "You're sure?"

"I'm positive."

"All right," Karen said slowly. "You're saying he was wearing that cast the night he died."

Eve nodded.

"But he could have taken it off; broken it off somehow."

Eve shook her head. "He could have. But I'm sure he didn't. You know what Ruth was like. She would have checked something like that out."

It was clear to all of them now. "So Raymond couldn't have used either of his hands. But somehow he knotted himself up a rope," Matt murmured. "Except he didn't. Because he couldn't have."

Eve, her eyes troubled, nodded. "But one of us could have."

Karen stared at her. "You don't mean that."

"It makes no sense," Buddy said angrily. "If Ruth had thought it was murder, why didn't she go to the police?"

"Maybe she did," Tim suggested. "Maybe they didn't believe her. Old man Becker was your prototypical pig-headed cop." He had another thought. "Or maybe Ruth thought she was protecting us. One of us."

"I wonder if that's why it never occurred to me," Eve said slowly. "Why I wouldn't allow myself to remember about Raymond's hand. Because I loved you all too much."

After a moment Buddy said, uneasily, "Not necessarily, Eve. It doesn't have to have been one of us."

"Oh, come on, Buddy. Who else could it have been?"

"You never know. A hunter. A camper. Or maybe no one. Maybe Raymond *did* hang himself."

"How?"

Buddy shrugged. "I don't know how. Okay, maybe he was crippled. But that only increased the odds of his not being able to do it. I mean, we're dealing with a human being here. We all know the infinite possibilities of a man; all the countless parts of him that can be realized if given the opportunity . . . all the handicaps he can overcome."

"It doesn't make any sense," Karen insisted,

almost angrily. "We barely knew him. What reason could we possibly have had to kill him?" She glanced away, trying to conceal the terrible, inexplicable disturbance she felt.

Eve shook her head. "I don't know. I don't know. I hope you're right." But it was obvious that she had no hope at all.

"I still think you're wrong, Eve," Buddy told her. "But I suppose if one of us did it, it'd have to have been the one who invited Raymond along that night."

"Assuming he didn't invite himself," Matt murmured.

When he spoke, Tim's voice was idle. "Okay, here's another thought. It came to me earlier tonight. If you guys are right—I mean, about all seven of us having been together only twice . . . that night at the lodge and then tonight—then isn't it odd? . . . Just two nights together. And each time someone got killed. Raymond the first time. Ruth the second."

They all shifted uneasily. Then Buddy nodded; his voice was casual as Tim's. "Now we're getting somewhere," he drawled. "If we can figure out who killed Ruth, then maybe we've got the one who murdered Raymond, too."

"Don't be ridiculous," Karen snapped. "None of us killed Ruth."

"Sam could have," Buddy said easily. "Could have snuck up the backstairs, done it, pitched himself out of a window, then scooted into the kitchen and back up the stairs." He turned to Sam. "Just kidding, of course."

They stared at him, shocked.

"Come on, man," Matt rasped. "We're just killing time here. No sense going too far with all of this."

"Thought I was making my contribution." Buddy shrugged. "Didn't want to get any of you uptight. Of course Sam didn't do it. None of us did. Either Raymond killed himself, or someone else did. Like someone else killed Ruth."

Karen felt sickened. *Sam.* He'd suggested that Sam . . . Buddy had always had a kind of sixth sense when it came to her; often could tell what she was feeling. And now he was trying to crush those feelings by voicing that . . . filth. She rose. "I have to go to the bathroom," she said.

Buddy sprang to his feet.

"Where are you going?" she asked.

"With you. Can't let you go up those stairs alone."

"Tim will come with me. Won't you, Tim?"

Looking uncomfortable, Tim nodded. "If you want me to," he told her, glancing from her to Buddy, then back.

Buddy exploded. *"Tim!* You can't be serious! Asking *Tim* to protect you from—from the beast who did all *that!"* The motion of his hand took in the bodies in the kitchen and upstairs.

Buddy had placed his free hand on her arm,

restraining her. Angrily she jerked away from him, and seizing Tim, drew him away with her.

The fire was burning low now, but no one noticed. Buddy lowered himself into a chair that faced the hall. Eve remained on the couch, sunk in reverie. After a moment Sam and Matt moved to one of the windows that faced toward the front of the property. There they watched the rain spring from the darkness outside and flail against the ancient panes.

"You think we're going to come out of this alive?" Matt asked in his casual way.

Sam's lips tightened. "Seems like we should," he said. "We've got the odds on our side."

For an instant the sky lit up, followed almost immediately by a crash of thunder. The window trembled in its setting. "Jesus," Matt whispered, startled. "Now lightning, too. The Devil's not missing a trick tonight." He turned to Sam. "I guess you're right," he said. "About the odds, I mean. But I've a feeling I'm not going to come out of this."

"You mean, now that the Devil's set his foot in it," Sam kidded softly.

Matt turned back to the window. He didn't look at Sam. "I believe in the Devil," he said simply.

"You can't mean that."

"I do." Matt's eyes were on him now, unflinching. Sam saw the truth there.

"I can't believe you. You're too intelligent for that."

"A lot of intelligent people believe in God. What's the difference between believing in God and believing in the Devil?" Matt didn't wait for an answer. "I feel the Devil is here with us tonight. I've felt it ever since we came."

Sam looked at him, stunned. There was no question Matt meant every word he said. Sam never would have suspected. What was it Buddy had said before? "The infinite possibilities of a man." There was a second part to that: *All the infinite parts of a man best kept hidden from the rest of the world.* He looked at Matt, not knowing what to say. Till now he'd always thought of him as a friend. Suddenly he didn't even *look* the same: It was as if he were a stranger, some stranger seen at three A.M. in a bus station. . . .

"But I don't much care," Matt went on, not noticing Sam's response. "You know, if I don't make it out of here. My reflexes are gone. Have been for a while, but I wouldn't admit it to myself. Racing's all I've ever cared about."

"What about your kids? All kids need a father."

Matt shrugged. "Too late now. I've been away from them too long to make up for all the lost time." He glanced at Eve. "Maybe I could have been a good father . . . maybe I could be still. If I'd had . . . you know, a woman like that."

Sam looked over at Eve. His eye traced the soft outlines of her cheeks, the gentle upward curve of her nose, the halo of brown-blond hair. He knew what Matt meant; there was a quality of womanliness, of kindness and receptivity in Eve that would attract most men. Attract them and probably hold them, too. He shrugged. "Maybe you can."

"What do you mean?"

"You can't tell me you haven't noticed. The way she's been throwing herself at you all night."

"You're crazy. She was only kidding around. She's not that kind of woman."

"I know. She isn't. But maybe there's something wrong. With her marriage, I mean. I'm telling you straight, Matt. I'd lay odds that she wants you."

There was another flare of lightning, and suddenly Sam, watching the light flash across Matt's face, found himself wondering what he'd done. Siccing a man who believed in the Devil onto Eve . . . But it was too late now.

9

She was so furious, she never thought of the danger as she stalked up the stairs. She'd been too angry to say anything to Tim. Not even when she shut the bathroom door and left him outside in the hall. Karen touched her forehead with her fingertips. It felt hot. Was it just rage, or was she becoming ill?

She grimaced. No, not ill. *Sick.* She was certainly sick. Sick of everything. All these years, trying somehow to make it work, feeling it was all her fault. It couldn't have been Buddy . . . he was too good, too perfect.

But she'd seen him tonight. Seen the real Buddy for the first time. He'd sensed what was happening with her. And hit her with the news of his failure; tried to tie her to him with that.

Then when that didn't work, he'd gone for the

groin, accusing Sam of Ruth's murder in that innocent-sounding voice of his.

She shook her head. *No.* That's your guilt making you say all that. Buddy's a good man. He always has been; has always tried to be; at times even desperately tries to be. He'd told her tonight because it was time. Now that he was on the brink of failure there was no time left.

The remark about Sam . . . She'd heard it as weakness. Had her guilt made her hear it that way? She'd always thought of Buddy as strong, indomitable, certain to overcome no matter what. And he *had* been strong. Wasn't he entitled to one moment of weakness? Especially after all these years of secret failure. The shame of it must have shattered him; had to have. Allow him that one slip . . .

Or had it been a slip? Maybe he'd just been mouthing off, like Tim, trying to keep the conversation going, trying to distract them from their situation. . . . And it had been her guilt that had made it seem like a slip.

Karen moved to the mirror, then quickly looked away, shuddering. *Damn* these candles—they made everything so grotesque. It was almost as if she'd seen her face as it would be in the grave, melting, distorted. . . .

She shook her head, a faint, rueful smile on her lips. What a night. Everything falling apart . . .

There was a flash of lightning, and for the first

time she could see outside. It was stark, uninviting, the trees skeletal, tortured; the ground bare, half dead, glints of black water in the distance.

Sam.

The pull was still there. She'd felt it as soon as she'd seen him tonight. It didn't surprise her. Had Buddy known all these years, sensed it? If so, what pain it must have given him . . . She closed her eyes wearily.

Finally she turned to the mirror, checked her makeup as best she could, then, as her hand touched the doorknob, paused. What was she stepping into? she wondered. Was she moving back to the life she'd always known, or was she taking her first steps into a whole new world, a world—she was sure now—she'd always wanted, a world she'd wanted despite the fact that it frightened her . . . ?

Tim nodded to her as she came out of the bathroom, and she found it was all she could do to nod back. There was nothing to say. They moved quickly down the narrow hall toward the staircase. As Karen reached the head of the stairs, she stiffened.

It was all mixed up with the sounds of the storm, and she had to listen for a moment till she could be sure. Then she turned to Tim in wonder. "They're singing!"

He nodded impassively, and she turned and started down the stairs.

"Well, you that I was a Tupelo man,
Spend all my money, that was your plan.
Have a lot of fun on my hard-earned
     jack . . ."

It seemed, under the circumstances, so bizarre.
Yet it filled her with hope. If they could sing, then
maybe things could be normal again, life could go
on. She found herself humming along, uncertainly at first, then more decisively.

Maybe when she was back in the room, being
with Buddy would feel right. Maybe, as Eve had
said, it was only tonight that it all seemed wrong
—skewed because of the kind of night it had
been. *Have I really always felt that way about
Buddy? About Sam?* Her confused thoughts
churned with the song and the storm until they
became so muddled that she pushed them out of
her mind.

She rushed in and finished the last bar of the
song with them. They were standing together in
the center of the room, all of them, Eve, Buddy,
Matt, Sam. "How's this for weird?" Eve asked her
cheerfully. "But we figured it'd be worth a try.
You know, at least drive off all the spooks who've
got taste in music." She turned to the others.
"How about 'Song Sung Blue'?"

They launched into that, and followed it with
"Day by Day." Karen noticed the fire was almost
out, but that wasn't important. As long as they
could keep the singing going, as long as they

could drive out all the crazed perceptions, the
fear . . .

It was Matt who started the next song:

> "I asked you, sweet baby,
>   Asked you to try, try, try . . .
>   Yes, I asked you, pretty baby,
>   To really get on down and try,
>   But you wouldn't do it for me baby."

And then:

> "Come on, Daddy's baby,
>   Throw down that last drop of rye
>   Because, see, pretty baby,
>   This's the time that we die . . ."

This's the time that we die. It struck all of them
at once. They tried to ignore it, to keep going, but
first one faltered, then another, until finally
they'd all fallen into silence.

Eve smiled uncertainly. "I've got to go upstairs.
You'll come with me, won't you, Matt?" She
didn't look at the rest of them as she hurried out
of the room. Matt trailed behind her, his expression thoughtful.

Karen glanced at Buddy, then at Sam. She
walked toward the front window. She barely
heard Sam the first time he spoke; he was too far
away, and his words were further obscured by
the crashing of a tree. But the urgency in his

voice was plain, and as she turned she heard him say it again. "Where's Tim?"

He was staring at her, his eyes intent. Crazily, she felt guilt flash through her. "I . . . I don't know. I thought he came back down with me. Didn't he? He was singing with us, wasn't he?" she asked fervently, as if the conviction in her voice could make it so. But she realized now that he hadn't been with them. Drawn by the singing, she'd forgotten all about him; hadn't thought about him from the time she was halfway down the stairs.

Eve washed her hands and opened the bathroom door. "Do you need to go?" she asked Matt.

Even in the flickering light his embarrassment was plain. He's like none of the rest of us, Eve thought. So bright, so surprisingly bright . . . and yet . . . something of the primitive about him . . . a lack of sophistication . . . "Actually, yeah," he said. "But I can't leave you out here."

"Don't worry about it," she told him. "I'm married, I have two boys. I'll turn my back."

As he pushed past her, apologizing, not looking at her, she smiled to herself. He was a brave, even reckless man. But he also had this other side. She stood with her back to him and waited for him to finish.

"All right," he said.

She turned to him, her arms raised and held out to him.

He responded as she'd known he would, instinctively. As his mouth came down on hers she felt as if she were being kissed for the first time; felt the sweetness of it, its wonder. . . .

Gently she drew her lips away from his. "You can have me," she told him. "I want you to have me. But I have to tell you this first . . ."

He was embracing her tightly, his gaze intent, his heart already pounding hard against her. He nodded and waited.

She gazed into his steady eyes and felt herself close to plunging into them. "I fell in love with you the first time I saw you, Matt," she told him. "Of course it was just a schoolgirl crush . . . as they say. But schoolgirl crushes aren't *'just.'* They're as deep and as real as any other kind of love. Mine was, anyway."

She raised one hand and touched his cheek. "And it never quite went away. Never. Even with marriage, even with the children . . . You don't know how often I thought of you. Some little part of me, hidden away . . . that part was always yours. And now lately . . . lately I've been thinking about you, thinking about you quite a lot. Through all these years, whenever I've fantasized . . . Well, it's always been you.

"I planned this long before tonight," she went on, "weeks ago. I didn't know how I was going to manage it, but I knew I would. Even with all that's gone on tonight, I still want to go through with it, to have you, just this once. I won't let anything take it from me. But I have to tell you first, tell you why—"

Her breath caught, and she had to halt. He waited, his eyes large, not questioning, not exactly that, but *ready*. The heat of his hands burned through her blouse.

She shuddered. "It's only this one time, Matt, it's only tonight. I'm sure that's okay with you, that that's all you'd want . . ." He began to shake his head, started to say something, but she wouldn't listen. *"Please.* I have to tell you this first. I have to make it very clear. I love my husband, Matt. I love my children. I'm going back to them. But first I wanted to have you. It was the only thing I regretted never having. See, I have to do it now, Matt. While there's time. What I mean is, I've only got a few months . . . I have cancer, Matt."

Too intent on what she was saying, she didn't notice his reaction; didn't feel his hands drop away. "It's not the bad kind," she hurried on. "Most cancers aren't the bad kind, did you know that? I didn't until . . . just a little while ago. They say it won't hurt. I'll just get weak. Weaker . . . I've already lost some of my strength, that's why I saw the doctor. . . . Just keep getting weaker . . . and then it'll be over. All ended. See? I'm going to be cheated out of so much . . . Growing old with my husband; seeing my kids grow up, go off to school, marry, have children. I'm going to lose all that, all of it. So this thing, at least this one thing, I want to have that. To kind of make up for . . . It'll give me something to think about, to hang on to as the time gets closer. . . ."

Matt lowered his eyes, then glanced up at her, shamefaced. He couldn't touch her. Not like that. She was Death. All the safety of her was gone.

Tears welled in her eyes. "Then hold me, Matt," she murmured. "Just hold me. For a little while. Let me have that."

She had to draw him to her, to clutch at him until finally he began to embrace her. Slowly his hands returned to her back, and soon she began to feel the heat of them again.

Matt followed her down the stairs, still shaken. He hadn't known how much he'd been hoping . . . until he'd found out there was no hope at all. He knew now: it could have been good, so very good. There might have been some point, some point to going on. . . .

She kept a few footsteps ahead of him, and when they entered the living room, she didn't look back at him. Was she ashamed? he wondered, and then cursed himself for his ego. What had happened between them could mean nothing to her. Not with what she was facing.

It took him a moment to understand what they were telling him. Something about Tim. They tried to mask the uneasiness, but it showed on all of their faces.

"He didn't say anything to you?" Matt asked Karen.

She shook her head, misery etched on her face.

"Not your fault," he tried to tell her. "*He* was looking out for *you*, not vice versa."

"No sign of him upstairs?" Buddy asked. Eve and Matt shook their heads.

When she spoke, Eve's voice trembled. "It doesn't mean anything, it *doesn't* . . . What happened to Ruth . . . Whoever killed her was probably returning for his weapon . . . to wipe off the fingerprints, hide it somewhere, destroy it. . . . I mean, it's *gone* now, isn't it? So that's all it was. Ruth had the bad luck to be there. But he's well on his way from here now. Tim's just gone off, you'll see, maybe to get firewood or something. He'll be back. He'll be *back*." Then she began to sob.

Everything in Matt strained to take Eve into his arms, to comfort her. He turned to Buddy. "You haven't looked for him yet?"

"Didn't want to chance it. Not till we had the two of you with us."

Sam moved out into the hall. "Tim!" he called, then shouted again. The only answer was the groaning of the house, the rattling of the windows, the shrieking of the winds. He swung back to them. "Looks like we're going to have to search."

10

Buddy and Sam led the way, the two women behind them, Matt bringing up the rear. On the second floor, the sound of the storm seemed closer than before, as if it were plunging through holes it had torn in the house. They went straight to the attic, the unspoken wish being that they'd find Tim there, wouldn't have to look into the room with the young girl again, wouldn't have to encounter Ruth's body another time on the backstairs, or be faced with the grotesquely sprawled corpses in the kitchen.

They went through everything as carefully as before, perhaps even more slowly, more apprehensively. By the time they were through, Sam found himself at a back window. His eyes flicked wide open. "Look!" he shouted.

Hearts beating wildly, they crowded around

him and peered out. In the midst of the swirling blackness there was a faint glow of light. "That wasn't there before," Buddy said.

Sam nodded, his eyes bright with hope. "You're right. We'd have seen it from the kitchen even if we'd missed it up here."

"Why would Tim be out there?" Eve asked, her voice small, as if not daring to hope.

"Why not?" Karen snapped, anxious for her guilt to be erased. "He might as well be there as anywhere."

"Sure. Maybe he decided he'd had enough of this house," Matt suggested. "Who knows? Maybe of us, too."

"If it *is* him out there," Buddy said slowly.

"Don't!" Karen cried sharply.

Buddy shook his head. "We've got to prepare ourselves. If we're going to go out there, we've got to be a hundred percent aware that it may not be Tim we'll be facing."

"We're going out there? Back into the storm?" Eve asked.

"We have to," Buddy told her. "We've got to know what's out there, whatever it is." He turned to the others. "Or don't you agree?"

Sam and Matt nodded. Karen said nothing. "But in case it *is* Tim out there," Sam added slowly, "let's remember to be careful on the way downstairs."

Matt waited with the two women while Sam and Buddy went to gather up the slickers they'd previously discovered in the back kitchen. The silence while the three of them waited was bad, but talking would drown out any sounds, and they had to stay alert.

Matt glanced at the two women. *Seem to be holding up. Don't look any rockier than the rest of us.* The strain on Buddy's face was very plain, and it came as almost a shock: It was the only time in Matt's memory he'd seen Buddy anything but totally confident.

Even under normal circumstances Matt was taut with nervous energy. Tonight he was stoked. He began to bob up and down. Something was going to happen. Soon. He was sure of that. It was the Devil's night. The Devil's night.

"Okay." Buddy's voice came through the kitchen door, an assurance that when it swung open there'd be no danger.

When they emerged, the two men were carrying three slickers and a sheet of canvas. They handed the slickers to Matt and the two women. "We've already decided," Buddy said, when Matt demurred. "Sam'll tie the canvas around his shoulders. I'd rather not have anything on. Feel freer that way."

They gathered up the tools they had chosen as weapons, then left by the front door. Buddy and Sam again led the way, with Matt guarding the rear. It was a struggle just to get down the porch stairs; the wind threatened to send them crashing back into the front of the house, and the rain drove at them like nails. When they rounded the corner and turned toward the back of the house, the rain no longer in their faces, it was a little better.

The darkness, though, was as bad as before. They had no light; the candles wouldn't have had a prayer, and they'd found no flashlights in the house. As they snaked along the side of the house, Matt strained to see the light they'd observed from the attic, but couldn't locate it. *Probably can't be seen from this angle. Or . . .*

The rain was fully on his back now, pounding at the slicker. Karen, just ahead of him, was barely visible. This darkness, he knew now, was the Devil's darkness. The certainty of it chilled him. But he kept on going, and then went off balance as he stumbled over something. In just the instant he spent recovering, he lost sight of Karen. *That's how bad it is,* he swore to himself. *Christ, she can't be more than a couple of feet ahead of me.* He pushed forward, moving faster now, trying to catch up, one hand sliding along the side of the house, keeping him oriented.

Then the house fell away. He was in the back. He could see it now, off in the distance, a glow that came and went. Probably a lantern. In a barn or shed. Then the light was gone, and he realized it was probably obscured by one of the party ahead of him. He'd found them again. He started to hurry forward, then stopped. Was that a voice? There, just off to his right . . . Maybe one of the others . . . There it was again. He began to move toward the sound.

There was a flash of lightning. Everything around him stood out starkly in the glaring white light. In that brief, flickering instant he stood frozen, wondering, even as he knew it was too late. . . .

There's nothing to be afraid of, Karen kept telling herself. *Eve's right. The killer only came back for his weapon, anxious to retrieve that clue. Poor Ruth just happened to be there at the wrong time. He's gone now; has been for hours. That's Tim out there, Tim who's out there with the light. Needed to be alone for some reason. That's Tim ahead, and there's no one else out here in the dark. . . .*

She forced herself to keep looking ahead; wouldn't allow her eyes to dart around each time there was a noise. Noises were everywhere: swooping, swirling, shrieking, tearing, snapping, crashing. She felt she couldn't take much more of it—the noise, the interminable pounding of the rain and wind. She wondered how long she'd have to be out here to be driven mad? She tried to turn it into a problem, something abstract. . . . Was the storm itself enough to push her into insanity, or did it need another element . . . this gnawing fear, this near-hysteria that was ready, at any second, to find itself facing an onrushing horror. Or did it need even more? Did it need a rupture between her and Buddy? Did it need

Sam's presence? She shook her head, trying to drive away the thoughts. But it was too late. Given an opening, the madness had stolen inside her, silently, insidiously, till now it almost overwhelmed her . . . all but one or two final shreds of common sense. *Tim's all right,* she told herself firmly. *Whoever committed those monstrosities is gone now; has to be. . . .*

They were getting closer. Karen could see that the light was coming from a window, glowing through four small panes. The shape of the building was lost in the storm, but she sensed it was a shed of some kind, a small barn. There was enough light so that, to her right, she could make Eve out now.

The sound of a voice. Someone was saying something, but she couldn't hear. She kept on, the shadows of the men ahead intermittently obscuring the light. They seemed to be heading straight for the window. Of course. They'd approach the window first. *Like in our teenage days.* Peering into a lighted room, knowing you could see inside perfectly, but if you kept back far enough, the person inside couldn't see you.

They halted by the window, Sam staring in, Buddy at her side now, clutching her by the elbow.

Sam's voice, exultant, came at them. "It's Tim. He's all right!" He began moving to his left, toward the front of the building. As the rest followed, Karen passed by the window. She looked in. Tim was seated on a rough-hewn wooden bench. His head was down. He seemed to be holding something.

Faint light filtered through the irregular cracks and knotholes of the shed's large weather-beaten door. "Tim! Tim! We're coming in!" Sam called before he entered.

The light from the lantern hanging from a rafter was surprisingly bright. Karen saw now what Tim was holding. It was a pistol, a small, very shiny automatic.

"Tim! For God's sake. What're you doing here? What's going on?" Sam cried.

Tim shook his head. "I couldn't do it," he said dully.

"Do what?" Then, when there was no reply, "Couldn't do what?"

"It's all a mess. None of it works. I'm still who I was. That's why none of it works of course."

Tim waved the pistol. "I've been carrying this with me . . . carrying it for weeks. Wanting to use it. Afraid to use it. Brought it with me. Just in case. In case things didn't work out. I still had hope when I was on my way here. Hope," he muttered wryly. "But it wasn't any different. It isn't. It never will be.

"And I'm not. Different, that is. I'm the same as I ever was. Should have known I couldn't use this damned thing. Stumbled out of the house like an idiot. All resolved to stalk off into the forest and put a bullet through the roof of my mouth. Splatter my brains up into the trees, let the rain wash them away . . ." He looked up at them, drained. "But I couldn't do it. I didn't have the guts."

He gave a short, humorless laugh. "And you know what? I thought that my wife's cheating on me was the last straw. I had this damn thing jammed halfway up my mouth when it came to me: I really don't *know* if she is cheating on me. She may not be. She really may not be. But she's so good-looking, so beautiful, I never could figure out why she'd married me, never been able to figure it. So I've never trusted her. I really don't have a shred of evidence, not a single shred. All I've got to go on is my paranoia. Not that it matters. That's not what stopped me."

Had the night shaken Tim as badly as it had her? Karen wondered. And then, suddenly, after all these years, she understood. He'd been "one of them." But he hadn't. They'd used him, all of them. Even Eve. Perhaps Eve more than any of them. After all, they'd dated, Eve thinking of him really only as a friend, an amusing companion, keeping him at arm's length.

Tim had been the unimportant one. Amusing, good company, but . . . unnecessary. And they hadn't been the only ones. All his life Tim had been reaching out for acceptance, love. When they were in the mood and his lines were on target, they laughed; included him in. She flinched as she thought of the times tonight when his jokes had been ignored, even sneered at. Tim the professor, the instructor in medieval religion, coming back, hoping to impress them . . . and they had treated him just as they always had. . . .

Tim's anguish was too stark, too naked for them. Shifting uneasily, Sam said, "We'd better be getting back to the house. It's a little too leaky in here."

Tim didn't seem to hear. "I don't have the guts —that's what stopped me. I just plain don't have the guts." For the first time he looked directly at them, his eyes moving listlessly from one to the next. "So at least it wasn't all wasted. I learned something. About myself." He began to rise, the pistol still in his hand. "Whatever happens, I'm going to stick around. Because that's all I can do. Because I don't have the guts to do anything else."

"Not too many have that kind of guts," Sam told him quietly. "Besides, don't you realize how important your life *is*? Jesus, you should have seen us, kid, thinking maybe somehow the—the the same thing that got Ruth—got you. You're important to *us*. One look at our kissers when we realized you were gone and you'd have known that. Hey, would we have come through all that crap flying around out there if we didn't think you were important?"

Tim's answering laugh was wry, but some life had returned to his eyes. He was coming back to them, coming back to the world. . . .

"This should make us all feel a lot easier," Sam

told him, gently taking the pistol from him. "Now we've got something better than a pick or a shovel."

"Won't do you any good." Tim shook his head wanly.

"What do you mean?"

"When I realized I couldn't do it, I took all the bullets out. Just to make sure. Flung 'em out there." He pointed in the direction of the storm.

Sam sagged a little. There wasn't a chance of finding any of them, not the way it was out there. "Well, we'd better go," he said quietly.

"Why?" Karen asked. "Why don't we just stay here?" She glanced at the snug confines of the shed. "It's only leaking in a few places. And it feels so much safer."

Eve nodded vigorously. Sam, eyeing them, said, "Maybe you're right."

And then, all at once, they noticed. Each of them.

Karen felt everything slip away. Matt had been behind her. Just as Tim had been before. She glanced around. Everyone in the group seemed to be staring at her. "He must have lost the way," she said anxiously. Suddenly the group—just five of them—seemed very small.

They waited for ten minutes. Then Buddy took the lantern off its hook. They'd head for the house. If Matt was still out there, still trying to reach them, he'd see the light, make his way to them . . . if he could.

11

As they left the shed and looked toward the house, the collective shock was almost palpable. When they'd first arrived, the house had been ablaze with light; now it was lost in the blackness of the storm. They'd left a few feeble candles burning in the front room; from here they could see nothing.

"We have to make a chain," Karen cried desperately. "We've *got* to hold tight to each other's hands. We *can't* let go."

"It wouldn't work. Not for the middle man, anyway." Buddy disagreed. He had the pick in one hand, the lantern in another. "He wouldn't have any way of hanging on to his weapons. Tim will lead, Sam'll bring up the rear. The four of you hang on to each other. I'll walk alongside Tim with the lantern."

They advanced that way into the storm, the rain slashing at their faces, their slitted eyes fixed on the ground, which was faintly illuminated by the lantern Buddy was carrying.

"Coming here, the rain seemed to be directly on our backs," Buddy shouted. "Probably if we just keep on facing into the wind . . ."

The lantern, Karen realized, made Buddy the logical first target, the most easily seen. If he were attacked first, the lantern would be smashed to the ground, everything would go black. Would the men try to help him, or would they seize that opportunity to protect the women by getting away, leaving Buddy on his own? Or might it happen so quickly that they'd *have* to run . . . too late to help Buddy? And if that happened— how would she feel? What would she do?

Did she really hate Buddy that much? *Hate* him? The idea had never occurred to her till now. Why should she *hate* him? Had she finally crossed over the border into insanity without knowing it? She had to be crazy to wish that what had happened to Ruth would happen to her own husband! One of her hands was gripping Sam's, and as his large, strong fingers closed over hers she felt a sudden urge to tear free, to flee from the shameful feelings that stirred inside her. . . .

Eve lurched through the dark, her body wracked with sobs. She was holding nothing back. The anger, the fear, the sadness—she let it all flow free. This night was only a continuation, a heightening, of the nightmare that had begun three months ago. It wasn't right, wasn't fair. She was such a good mother, such a good wife, and it was all being taken from her. Her grandparents had lived into their nineties, her mother and father were still alive and healthy. Who was it who'd learned Greek at the age of eighty? She'd once decided that when she was eighty she'd do that too . . . had laughed to herself about it, amused, smug. . . . She'd felt so sure, so invulnerable. . . .

Death was for other people. She'd barely thought about it . . . it was too far off. There were too many other things and people to think about, to care for. . . .

Raymond. Evil doesn't die. It doesn't *die*. It's like a fungus, feeding on living things. She was sure of that, wholly certain, now, that she'd learned to know evil intimately, aware it was growing inside her own body, quietly, insidiously. And Raymond *had* been evil. She'd sensed it even then; had been repelled by it; shied away from it. And yet . . . she'd been drawn to it. How many times had she found herself watching him, unable to take her eyes off him? And then his gaze would catch hers, and there would be that look, that look of something secret, hidden, something that only he knew about, something sly, subterranean, *evil*. That evil was here tonight, and it was going to take them all.

The irony of it was unbearable. It wasn't right for this to happen to her—to someone who was already counting the few precious days remaining to her . . . To be cheated even of that. She was shaken by a paroxysm of sobs, and then . . . nothing. All at once she realized, startled, that there was nothing left inside her. Nothing. She was emptied, barren, like a house before a move. Things thrown out, given away . . . no need for them anymore. . . .

Eve had stopped, and Karen, fiercely gripping her hand, saw that it was because Buddy had stopped. A huge tree was lying across their path. Instead of going around, Buddy was looking for an opening.

The branches were thick, almost impenetrable. Buddy moved off to the left and they followed. A few steps on, he stopped and raised the lantern high, indicating a place he thought passable.

Tim had already helped Eve over when Sam came up alongside Karen. He stepped over the tree with her, then advanced a few feet and reached out for Buddy, who was about to go on. He was shouting into Buddy's ear. The shattering sound of the wind kept the words from Karen, who was barely a foot away. But she saw Buddy nod and turn back toward the tree as he grabbed Tim and shouted to him. Had they found Matt? Had he been felled by the tree?

If only it were that simple . . . a natural force,

an act of nature . . . nothing more than that. He'd be all right, of course . . . conscious, not badly hurt. The men would pick him up. She and Eve would help them get him back to the house. . . .

But they found nothing. They walked the length of the tree, first one side, then the other; but there was no sign of Matt, and soon they were struggling against the storm again, making their way toward the house.

Karen couldn't see any of their faces, but she could picture them. The glint of hope gone, apprehension taking its place. Could anyone have had the thoughts that she had? Was it normal . . . to hope that a friend had been struck down by a tree? As they fought their way into the storm, she found herself wondering if they were walking in a circle, the way people did when they were lost. The wind was still in her face, but that didn't necessarily mean anything. It could have shifted. It was constantly shifting, coming from the front, then the left, then maybe the right, and then the front again. Easy to become confused, to be thrown off . . .

But then Eve's pace slowed, and as Karen came up to her she heard her shout, and then saw it. The house was there, in front of them. Her heart skipped a beat. They'd made it. But where was Matt? What were they walking back into?

Was he in the house? Had he wandered off in the wrong direction, then decided to make his way back alone and wait for them? Yes, that was it. It made the most sense. Tim had been all right. Matt would be, too. She turned to look back at Sam, to communicate the reassurance she'd just felt. Her movement brought her right foot out to the side, and suddenly she felt herself falling.

She hit, and as she did, the fingers of one hand struck something that gave way. Down they plunged, into something liquid, something warm and sticky. Immediately she knew what it was. She screamed and wildly threw herself away from Matt's tortured remains, frantically slashing her hand back and forth over the rain-soaked grass, desperately trying to rid herself of the blood and bits of him that clung to her. In the dim light of the approaching lantern, Sam saw and understood. Swiftly he drew out a handkerchief and savagely swiped at her hand, over and over again, ferociously attacking whatever traces might be left. As he dropped beside her she whirled to him and buried her face against his chest, clinging to him as he pulled her to her feet.

She kept her face turned away even when the others joined them. Buddy raised the lantern high. Eve clutched at Karen, and the two women clung together in a desperate embrace, supported by Sam, as slowly Buddy moved the lantern, letting its light travel the length of Matt's body.

Sickened, stunned, they looked at each other for a moment, then turned toward the house.

There was no question about moving the body, and this time it had nothing to do with the law. It would have taken two men. Leaving a lone man to defend the group was suddenly unthinkable.

12

There was no sense of relief when they reached the front door. They exchanged mute glances in the moment before Sam opened the door. Who knew what might leap out at them or, just as likely, attack them from behind even before they could get inside? The moment they were all in, Buddy quickly pushed the door to and bolted it. *No!* Karen wanted to cry out. *No, don't do that! What if it comes at us—what if this is our only way out?* But she was afraid of sounding hysterical and foolish, afraid of sounding like a hysterical and foolish woman.

Eve staggered into the living room. There was no feeling of having found sanctuary. The evil she'd sensed before was still with them. She glanced toward the fire. There was nothing now but a few embers. The light from the lantern wasn't nearly as effective in here. But rebuilding the fire would mean that two of the men would have to go out for wood, one gathering, one guarding. . . .

All but two of the candles had melted down. "Are there any more?" she asked.

Karen shook her head. "Not in here. I looked."

"The dining room?"

"Not there, either."

Raymond. She felt his presence now, more than ever. He'd be grinning, leering at them the way he used to leer at her. . . . She dropped onto the couch, her face in her hands.

Karen, seeing Eve's reaction, turned toward the three men. Tim's upper lip appeared to be trembling, and Buddy was agitated in a way she'd never seen him before. His movements were abrupt, hesitant, erratic.

Only Sam seemed unshaken. When their eyes met, the look he returned was quiet, reflective. A moment later he began moving the furniture. "How about giving me a hand?" he called to Buddy and Tim. "We can move the dining-room table in here."

They didn't understand. "If he tries to come in here," Sam explained, "the more stuff we have piled between him and us, the tougher it'll be for him to get to us. It'll give us an edge."

Tim nodded, and followed Sam into the dining room. Buddy picked up a small table, then stopped, set it down, and stood unmoving, his gaze far off, disoriented.

Sam and Tim brought in the big table, maneuvering it so that it stood at an angle between the hall and the front section of the living room. With a quizzical glance at Buddy, Sam took the small table and added it to the other furniture, creating an extension to the barricade formed by the dining-room table.

Tim seemed bewildered about what to do next, but Sam went on, carrying in a large, threadbare wing chair, walking over a small bookcase with the books still on the shelves, jamming the dining-room chairs against the large table, like shields at the side of an ancient fighting ship. There was only one piece of furniture left, an easy chair. He dragged it across the room until it stood near the narrow passageway he'd left in the barrier.

"Guess you'd better scrunch yourselves through," he said, examining his handiwork. "I want to plug this thing up now."

Wordlessly they followed his suggestion. Once they were in, Sam drew the chair after them. "All right," he said, "that should slow the bastard down a little."

"Not if the bastard comes in through the windows," Tim said, trying to make a joke of it, but his eyes were white and wild, like the lightning that flashed as he spoke.

Sam had already considered it. "Storm windows are up. That makes two layers of glass. Mess him up pretty good if he tries it. I figured we could slap up a couple of boards to help out. But that'd mean searching around out back."

"So this is it?" Buddy said, breaking his long silence. The two women were huddled on the couch. The men were standing, half facing the hall. Sam had gathered up the weapons. He had the shovel in his hands. The pick lay near Tim, the poker and sickle near Buddy. Buddy's voice, like Tim's, showed strain. "We sit here behind these sticks of furniture, waiting to be attacked?"

"If you've got a better idea, let's have it," Sam told him.

Buddy turned away.

Karen, hearing the sound of her own voice, realized she must be in shock. "Wouldn't it be better if we didn't talk? So we can be ready . . . hear the first sound . . . ?" The words came out so slowly, so dully.

Eve shook her head. "It doesn't make any difference. It doesn't make any difference whether we speak or not. It doesn't make any difference about the furniture, either, about trying to protect ourselves. Can't you tell?" she whispered. "It's Raymond."

"Don't talk nonsense," Buddy snapped. "Raymond's dead."

"Yes, he's dead." Eve's head dropped, and her voice became a whisper. "But it doesn't make any difference."

"What in God's name are you talking about?" Buddy cried. Karen stared at him. She'd never seen him like this: He seemed very near hysteria.

"The evil," Eve responded without emotion. "The evil Raymond left behind. It's been with us all night. In the car, in the storm, in this house . . ."

Disgust etched itself in Buddy's face. But Eve persisted. There was no fear in her expression; only fatigue and resignation, as if it were too late for fear. "You don't understand. You can't," she said tonelessly. "But I'm . . . I'm no longer the same. Haven't been for a while. Because of it, I find myself in touch with . . . other things. Things I'd never been aware of before. Things from . . . well, from another place."

She looked up at them. "That sounds quite mad, doesn't it? But I'm not mad. I know I'm not. Do I look mad? Do my eyes look mad?" she asked, gazing at them calmly.

Suddenly Karen knew. It was as if, from the first instant she'd seen Eve tonight, she'd known. This was a night for truths. She didn't hesitate. "You're dying, aren't you?" she asked.

Eve's shoulders drooped. One hand fluttered toward her lips, then, just as quickly, dropped. All at once she looked very small, very frightened.

"It's all right," Karen told her softly. "You can tell us. It's better if you do."

Eve nodded, swaying as if in pain. "I've wanted to tell you . . . all of you . . . but most of all you, Karen. I need so desperately to tell. But I was afraid," she continued, shaking her head wearily. "I was afraid that if I told . . . you'd begin to blame all of this on me. You know, as if somehow this obscene thing inside me could touch everyone who came in contact with me. . . ." Her eyes shut. "Maybe it *does*. It touched Matt. And I told *him*. He was the one person I told."

She began to sob. Karen drew Eve toward her, cradling her head against her breast.

"Maybe she's right," Tim burst out. "Maybe Raymond's spirit *has* been with us all night. But maybe now he's gone. Maybe now that *Matt's* dead, *it's* gone."

"What do you mean?" Buddy's voice seemed filled with hope, a hope born of desperation.

"I mean, maybe it was Matt who hung Raymond. Maybe Raymond was suing Matt's folks, or going to. For the accident. Or maybe Matt had some kind of secret. Maybe Raymond was blackmailing him with it. Raymond was like that. You could see him doing something like that. But now . . . now that Matt's dead . . . Well, maybe now it's all over. It probably *is* all over," he finished, desperately.

Eve drew away from Karen. She looked up at Tim. "No," she said quietly, "it wasn't Matt."

The rain hammered against the windows as a violent gust shook the house. When it died down,

Karen asked, trying to keep the apprehension out of her voice, "Why do you say that?"

"Because I feel Raymond in this room. *Now.* He wouldn't still be here if the one he wanted was Matt."

Sam's gaze swept the group. Matt's belief in the devil, Eve's insistence on an evil spirit, Tim's going along with it—obviously shaken all over again by what Eve had just said. He could see that Karen was on the verge of losing her grip. He shook his head; forced conviction into his voice. "We're going to get through this. I promise you," he said, seemingly directing his words to Eve, but hoping they would have an effect on everyone.

Tim's response was immediate. "Oh, yeah?" he cried, his voice hysterical, "You have some kind of guarantee? You think you're safe, do you, just because we piled up some furniture? Tell me, what the hell do we do when these last two candles have burned out, when the kerosene's used up? What do we do when we're attacked by something we can't even see, something that's already taken out a guy as tough and as strong as Matt? Torn him up as if he were nothing? Tell me, how do we fight that?"

"We'll be all right," Sam doggedly repeated. "There're five of us. Just one of him. We'll be all right as long as we stick together."

"Stick *together*? Seems to me you all *were* together when you came out looking for me! A hell of a lot of good that did Matt!"

Karen jumped to her feet. "Shut up! Shut up!" she cried. She couldn't shake the illogical feeling of guilt, the same guilt she'd felt when Tim had disappeared. Matt had been just behind her. . . . She should have known, been aware of what was happening, saved him somehow. He'd been behind her to protect her; had died to save her. . . . "I can't listen to all this!"

But Tim couldn't be stopped. "Did you see him?" he asked, his voice low, his eyes hollows. "Did you see what he looked like? That's what's going to happen to *us*! To *all* of us!"

"Don't," Sam warned. "You're only making it worse."

A grotesque semblance of a laugh jerked out of Tim. "*I* can't make it any worse." He pointed in the direction of the hall, his voice high-pitched and shrill. "*That's* what's going to make it worse!"

Sam's hand slammed against Tim's throat. "Stop!" he told him, his voice dangerous. Instantly Tim subsided. He slid down the wall till he was seated on the floor, facing the couch, his back against the stone facing of the fireplace. For what seemed an endless time, they sat wrapped in tense silence. It was Karen who suddenly broke it, asking, "How long can this storm go on?" The wind and the rain were as wild as ever.

"I don't know," Sam answered wearily. "With a hurricane, there's no way of telling."

"It's the storm, that's what it is," Karen exclaimed. "It's not Raymond, it's the storm," she rushed on, as if by saying it forcefully enough she could exorcise the insanity that was choking the room. "If it hadn't been for this damned storm, none of this would have happened. Do you realize that? It's all *chance*, all a matter of *chance*. If it weren't for the storm, we never would have come here. Ruth would be alive, Matt would be alive. We'd be home now, in our beds. . . ." And then, abruptly, she stopped, realizing that she didn't *want* to be home in her bed. Not anymore. Not if it was a bed she shared with Buddy. She glanced at Sam, wondering if he could read her feelings. Then she looked at Buddy. Was that hate she saw in his eyes? Or fear? Or was it just her fevered imagination, fueled by the flickering lights that warped the truth of everything they fell on? She shut her eyes in anguish.

Buddy's voice, when he spoke, was its normal well-modulated baritone. "Tim was right about the fire. We need more light." When no one responded, he went on: "If two of us went for wood, it'd probably be all right. Two against one should be all we'd need. And if we heard shouts coming from here, we could run back in time. Nothing could happen that fast."

"No!" Karen cried. "Better to burn the furniture!"

"Need it for protection," Sam murmured.

"Then I'd rather wait here in the dark, knowing we're all together. My God, if you were out there, you couldn't hear us shouting, not in this storm!"

Ignoring her, Buddy said, "Let's go, Tim. You and I can do it."

Tim shook his head. "I'd rather not," he said shakily. He looked pathetic.

"Sam?"

"I'm against it. As important as the light is, it's more important for us to keep together. Two of you against a man with an ax: the odds are debatable. The five of us against him . . . some of us would be sure to survive."

"Then we'll use the furniture for firewood."

"No good."

"Who the hell are you to tell us what to do?" Buddy picked up a table and smashed it against the brick fireplace.

"Don't," Sam told him. "No more."

"Who appointed you leader? I'll do whatever I damn please."

Sam's voice was strained. "I'm asking you, Buddy. Leave it alone."

"Screw you." Having fed the splintered wood into the fireplace, he picked up one of the wooden chairs.

"Don't. *Please,*" Sam implored, laying his hand on Buddy's shoulder.

The next instant he reeled back as Buddy's fist crashed against his jaw.

Before he could recover, Buddy was on him, throwing him back onto the table, then leaping on top of him, aiming blows to his head. Sam twisted, slipping the blows, then raised his feet and pushed hard, throwing Buddy back.

"Let it alone," he cried. But Buddy, who'd fallen, was already back on his feet and coming at Sam.

Buddy was a natural athlete, Sam was lithe and sinewy, with surprisingly powerful arms. They traded blows, the thud of their punches resounding through the room. "Stop! Stop!" Karen screamed. Eve screamed, too, her fearful eyes on the now undefended doorway.

One of Buddy's punches sent Sam staggering back against the fireplace wall. But as Buddy came at him, Sam shot out his right arm, catching Buddy flush on the chin. Buddy's legs went rubbery. Sam leapt into him, his fists slashing at Buddy, once, twice, a third time . . .

Buddy went down, and Sam backed off. But as Buddy came up he had something in his hand. It was the poker. He raised it over his head. . . .

"No! No!" Tim jumped between the two men, waving wildly. "Stop! It's all right! We're all right now! *The storm's over!*"

The five of them turned toward the windows. Tim was telling the truth. There was no sound of wind, no spatter of rain. The night was totally, wholly silent. Eve began to sob.

"We can get out of here now," Tim cried. "Thank God, we can get out! See? The moon's

out! We'll be able to see, to find our way
back. . . ."

"No."

They'd all begun to stir. The urgency in Sam's
voice froze them.

"It's a hurricane, remember? That's what the
warnings were about all day, a hurricane. *This*
doesn't mean anything. We're only half out of it.
Sitting in the eye now. The second part can hit us
at any time. And when it does, it'll be even worse.
That's the way hurricanes work."

"Are you crazy?" Buddy rasped. "You're telling
us to stay here?"

"Yes."

"Sorry," Tim said. "I can see outside. I can see
and I'm going to get *out* of here while I can see.
Because soon all you're going to have in this room
is moonlight. And when the second half hits—*if* it
hits—then you're not even going to have that."

"We're surrounded by water," Sam said, desperately. "You'll still be cut off, still be vulnerable."

"Maybe. But maybe it's already beginning to
drain off. And if not, we can still get far enough
away from the house, find something we can float
on, pole our way away from here. . . ."

"And what if you can't?"

"I'll still be out of this house. Even if the storm's
twice as bad as before, I'll still be safer out there
than I am in here."

"Come on, Karen," Buddy told her, extending his hand. His blond hair was glowing in the soft light, and his face looked strangely calm.

"I'm not going," she said.

His eyes widened. "What do you mean, you're not going?"

She didn't answer.

"Dammit, Karen, I said come on!" Buddy's voice was angry. Sam edged a bit between the two of them. "If you stay," Buddy continued, "you'll be left alone. With him."

"I'm not going," she said again.

"Dammit—Eve?"

"I'm going to stay."

Buddy stared at her.

She shook her head. "I can't face the storm again. Not if it's going to be worse."

"Look," Sam reasoned, "if you two are thinking of going, what about our boy? Don't you think he may be on the move now, too? This is *his* chance to get away."

"You may be right," Tim said tightly. "But I can't take it in here anymore. I know I should stay. Help protect you. But I can't. I've got to get out of here. Come with us. All of you."

Karen looked at Eve, then at Sam. "We're staying," she said.

"It's your goddam lives," Buddy murmured savagely. He turned to Tim. "Come on, let's go!"

As they left, Tim with the sickle in one hand,

the shovel in the other, Buddy carrying the poker, one of the candles sputtered out. Karen sprang over to it, but it was no use. There was nothing left to revive.

13

As they came down the front stairs, Tim glanced to his right. "Look!" he whispered. "A garage. With a truck!"

Because of the darkness, they hadn't seen it before. They hurried over, Buddy murmuring, "Careful."

When they reached the door of the garage, weapons ready, they stopped. Tim shook his head dolefully. "He must have done this first," he said, pointing to the slashed tires. "So they couldn't get away."

"We may be able to use it anyway. Just ride it on the rims." Cautiously Buddy advanced into the garage and raised the truck's hood. "No use." He shrugged. "He did a nice job on the engine, too."

They headed back to the driveway. The air was

as still and oppressive as when they'd left the reunion. Tim sniffed. There was a faint smell of the sea. "So it was real," he muttered. "We really *were* smelling the ocean."

At the top of the long, slanting drive, Buddy decided: "We'll head straight down to the road. If it's impassable there, we'll just have to scout around. Bound to be a way out of here. There's an answer to everything. There always is."

Tim said nothing. The stillness was almost unsettling, so marked a contrast to what they'd endured before. The moon was full, sharply etching the fallen trees and limbs that littered the grounds. He turned back to look at the house. It was the first time he'd really seen it. It had been masked before by black night and swirling rain. Now it should simply have looked like an old New Jersey farmhouse. Instead, he felt a chill run through him as he realized the house, as it stood revealed by the moonlight, filled him with foreboding. Choosing words that would make his question seem light, he edged closer to Buddy. "You're keeping your eyes and ears peeled, aren't you?"

"Don't worry. There's no way he can take us, not in all this moonlight. No matter how strong he is, how insane he is, as long as I can see him first, he's gone. I can parry anything he comes at me with. And when he's open, I'll get him with this." He pointed to the angled end of the poker.

"And while he's still rocky, you come at him with the shovel, or the sickle."

Tim nodded rapidly, wondering what, in fact, he *would* do. Stand and fight? Run? Or simply freeze, too terrified to move? He thought about the wasted ammunition lying somewhere outside the shed; wondered if it wouldn't have been easier after all if he'd pulled the trigger . . . before he had the chance to find out just how deep his cowardice went. To fail at suicide was one thing. To abandon a friend . . .

In spots the thoroughly soaked ground was pure mud. Every time he sank into it, water leaked into his shoes. It was cold and unpleasant, and they'd barely begun. Yet anything was preferable to the horror they'd left behind. He thought of Sam and Karen and Eve. Sam was strong and quick; he'd beaten Buddy. He'd protect the women; they'd come out all right. And if not . . . well, dammit, they'd had their chance. They could have come along. It wasn't his fault they hadn't.

Somewhere behind him a twig snapped. He whipped around, his heart frozen. "Stop!" he whispered to Buddy, then watched, his eyes darting nervously. But there was nothing—nothing he could see. "All right." He nodded uncertainly. "Let's go." He found himself wishing he hadn't let the women off so easily. He should have argued with them, persuaded them. Even if Sam had remained behind, the four of them together . . . Safety in numbers . . .

They were almost at the end of the driveway. Buddy stopped and pointed. "Look."

The road and everything beyond was completely covered by water. "Let's keep along the edge of this till we find something," Tim said. "I want to stay as far away from the house as we possibly can."

Buddy nodded. "Absolutely. We're out of all that, and we're *staying* out of all that." He jerked his head to the right. "Let's try this way. Probably we're better off heading toward Thirty-one than going back the way we came."

As they slogged alongside the flood, Tim found he was beginning to relax, was paying more attention to the condition of his feet than to the shadows around them. It helped having Buddy as a companion of course. Golden Boy. Nothing had ever seemed to touch Buddy, nothing bad, nothing unlucky. The grace of his body, the grace of his nature, seemed to produce an aura that was like a shield. Nothing bad ever happened to Buddy, which meant if you were with him, you'd be all right, too.

Of course, that hadn't been the case tonight. More than one fall from grace for Buddy tonight. But it was understandable, under the circumstances. And now that they were out of it, Buddy was his old self. It was stupid, of course, to grab on to something like this, Tim told himself. But the

way things had been going, any straw seemed
worth grasping at.

As they walked Tim began to get a sense of the
land around them. The house was situated on top
of a small mound-shaped hill, almost perfectly
round from top to base. Of course, that was from
this angle, from the front. It might be different in
back. There'd been no way of telling what it was
like before, when he'd started walking away from
the house and found himself stumbling into a
shed. Perhaps the land back there was higher;
formed a sort of bridge that would lead them
somewhere, to another road, another house . . .

He sniffed at the air. Was the smell of the ocean
getting more intense now? The scent of it when
they'd left the gym had been a clue to what was
coming, the advance rider. And if it really was a
hurricane, if they were in the eye of it now, if the
intensity of the smell *was* increasing, then how
much time did they have?

He turned to Buddy. "You smelled the ocean as
soon as we came out of the house, too, didn't
you?"

Buddy nodded.

"How about now? Does it seem stronger?"

Buddy took a breath. He shook his head. "No,
it's about the same."

Tim began to relax again. If Buddy saw no difference, then there probably was none. His spirits rising, he nearly started to whistle, catching
himself just in time. He looked to his side. They'd

soon be on a line with the house. A minute or two more and they'd find out if there was high ground . . . or if they were stranded. The idea of finding something they could float on, pole their way to safety on, suddenly seemed like less than a good idea. Even with the moonlight, it was too dark, the way too uncertain, too tangled with fallen trees. Who knew what rapids they might find themselves in, unable to see ahead, not knowing whether in two hundred feet, a hundred, twenty, they might suddenly discover they were nearing the crest of a falls. . . .

No. No sense thinking like that. He had to wait, concentrate on finding high ground. And if he didn't . . . Well, he'd deal with that when they got to it. He looked toward the house. It should have called up images of comfort and warmth, dry shoes and socks, but he was experiencing no second thoughts. . . . *If the storm hits again, if I can take all the pounding of the wind and the rain, then dammit, I'll stay out here. . . . Hell, a hurricane coming could be a blessing. I'd probably be safer than I am now. No way I'd have to worry about an ax coming at me. Damn. Push* that *thought out of the way, pal. Forget about all that. Just concentrate on finding a way out of here . . .*

Suddenly he could see the shed, angled off to his right. *Site of the famous suicide attempt,* he thought with grim humor. He found himself wondering if Buddy had ever thought of suicide. *Talk about impossible. The Golden Boy thinking about taking that Golden life . . . Still, as they say, you never know. What was that poem again? The one about the guy everybody envied who one day put a bullet through his head. Never could remember the name of the damned thing . . . That's why I teach history instead of English. . . .*

"Listen!" Buddy's voice was hushed, strained.

Tim's heart sank, his eyes darting in every direction. Then he realized what Buddy meant. He could hear it, off in the distance, a faint roar. "Do you think it's . . ."

"The rest of the hurricane? Yes." Buddy nodded. "Come on, let's start running. We've got to find a way out before it reaches us."

The faster and harder they ran, the wetter they became; splashing through puddles, plowing through rain-heavy underbrush that drenched them. As they trampled the branches and twigs that littered the ground, they made a hell of a racket. Unlikely anyone was out here, but if he was . . . Running forward at full tilt, Tim found himself glancing desperately to the rear.

But at the same time hope began to bubble up inside him. They were past the grounds of the house, had entered a woods, and so far there was no water. Perhaps they had found high ground; it would be all right now. Might take them a while to stumble back into civilization, but at least they weren't stranded, still trapped in that nightmare. . . .

Buddy was pulling ahead of him. Reluctant to call out, Tim, trying to increase his speed, threw himself out of synch. He lost his balance, staggered forward a few steps, then lurched to the side. His hands went out as he hit the ground, the sickle and shovel flying.

Christ! The pointed end of a branch projected up from the water-soaked earth. One of his hands had driven hard into it. He tore his palm free, began to inspect it, then stopped in mid-motion. Their running had covered up the sound, but he heard it now. It was no longer a faint roar; it sounded like a freight train tearing over the back of the hill, heading toward the woods, toward *them.* Forgetting his hand, he jumped to his feet. He could still see Buddy ahead of him. "Wait! *Wait!*" he shouted, hoping Buddy would hear, praying his plea wouldn't be smothered by the terrifying sound of the oncoming storm.

Then it hit.

The noise was incredible. The wind and rain came at him like a wall, the impact of it throwing him face-first into the tree ahead of him. At any other time he would have crumpled and fallen to the ground, but in that first stunned instant the wind pinned him against the trunk.

The pain was terrible; broken nose, he guessed as he slid down the length of the tree trunk and then crawled around behind it, trying to protect himself from the wind. Sam had been right: as bad as the first part of the hurricane had been, and it had been the worst he'd ever seen, it didn't compare to this. The sound of it was terrifying; in the tearing wind the nearby trees were shuddering and snapping.

The pain was excruciating; he moaned and sobbed as he huddled behind the tree. Yet, he told himself, if his nerves held out, if the tree held up, he'd be all right here. Safe. With the wind as it was, it was unlikely any of the nearby trees would hit him if they fell; they'd be toppled straight forward.

He had no hope of Buddy's reaching him. The poor guy was just as trapped; maybe had already been hurt, even killed by a falling tree or hurtling branch. He could hear things thudding and crashing into the other side of the trunk; could feel the impact as they struck. He moaned again; in his pain and fear he was losing all sense of time. It was as if time no longer existed, as if what was now would always be.

He found himself thinking of the three back in the house. Were they safe? They might be dead now, all of them. He thought of Eve. Poor Eve, so terrible for her even if she survived all this . . . They say you never quite stop loving the first one. He never had, not quite. And it wasn't just the residue of a foolish schoolboy infatuation. . . . Eve deserved to be loved; *deserved* it.

Now she was going to die, might already be

dead, along with the others. Buddy, too, maybe. Of the seven who came here tonight, I may be the only one left.

What if it's true? Me, the one who'd always envied all the others. Ironic. Hard to feel sorry for myself ever again if it turns out that way. I will anyway, of course; it's too much a part of my nature by now. It's my fate; doomed always to be the wisecracking friend of the hero, the good-natured sidekick who secretly wishes the hero were dead, or hideously deformed, crippled, pov-erty-stricken. Good old Tim. Always good to have around. If only they'd known . . .

Incredibly, the wind seemed to be strengthen-ing. The tree had begun a continuous vibration. *What if it goes down? Will I be able to get out of the way, or will it crush me, drive me into the ground? Or pin me here, half alive? Will that be the way I end, lying here, battered by a hurri-cane, feeling my life leaking out of me, wet, cold, alone?*

He pushed the thoughts away. *Pointless. Think of something that'll get your mind off where you are, make you less aware of the chaos around you.* He forced himself to think back to the early days, back to his childhood. They'd known each other almost from the start, most of them. He and Buddy and Karen and Eve had been friends al-most forever, it seemed. Even at a time when other boys would have nothing to do with girls, Karen and Eve had often been part of their group, playing tag and hide-and-seek, swimming . . .

He began to lose himself in his thoughts, only half aware of the sound of the pelting rain, the swirling wind. He was seeing their high school days now: Ruth becoming a part of the group for the first time, dim remembrances of gradually becoming aware that Raymond was part of the class, then Sam's first day at the school. That still stood out. You noticed Sam right away. Something about him made everyone notice him, watch him, feel drawn to him. He'd seen it all over again tonight, the way Ruth had looked at Sam. Karen, too? Hard to believe, with Buddy, her husband, her lifelong love, at her side; but it had looked that way. . . . Or was he just being envious again? Whatever it was Sam had, he'd never had, never come close.

Raymond . . . He saw him again in gym—gray face, gray outfit. . . . He'd never noticed anything wrong with his arm, but then he hadn't been looking. Ruth's ideas about Raymond's death . . . Absurd, of course. Could be that it hadn't been suicide, grant her that—that'd he'd been killed. By someone else. Someone who'd found him there after they'd left, or maybe even while they were there. Maybe the same maniac who was on the loose tonight . . . someone who needed to kill. He thought about Raymond; tried to hear his voice . . . couldn't, really. They'd barely ever spoken. Maybe never had. He tried to remember all the times he'd seen him, whom he'd seen him with. But he'd always been alone. Every time. Or . . . Suddenly it came to him. A flash of memory. A fragment, but very clear. There *had* been times Raymond hadn't been alone. And now he remembered something else. The corpses in the kitchen . . . that glimpse of Matt's ravaged body . . . He rolled onto his side and squinted into the wind through his rapidly swelling eyes. There was probably nothing to it. Probably. And then he remembered what Eve had said about the evil of Raymond. Again his mind went back to that flash of memory, and for the first time he understood. He *had* to get back to the house.

One hand shielding his eyes, he began to crawl forward into the wind. Lightning flashed and he looked up. In that instant he could see ahead of him; could see the few trees that remained between him and the clearing; could see the shed and house beyond. He could make it. With just a little luck he could make it back to the house.

He wriggled his way forward, yearning to break free of the trees, anxious to be able to get to his feet and run toward the house. Was it envy driving him? Was that all it was: the wish finally to give vent to his blackest dreams, his most shameful desires?

Something flew at him and tore his cheek. He raised his hand and felt the gash, deep, long. . . . Maybe he was wrong. Even if he was right, it could already be too late. How inviting the comfort and safety of the tree seemed now. But he continued to crawl forward, his elbows all mud, his underside becoming soaked through, the rest of him already drenched.

Another flash of lightning, and he saw he was already in the clear. His heart pounding, he rose to his feet . . . and instantly found himself thrown to the ground. He tried again, this time slanting so much into the gale that his head was barely three feet from the ground. But as he pushed into it the wind's force supported him, and he began to stagger forward, every part of the body besieged. The stinging assault on his face was ceaseless; he couldn't tell how much of it was rain and how much small projectiles tearing into his flesh.

He'd been heading into the wind, estimating how far he had to go before he drew abreast of the house. Now, hoping he was right, he turned to his left, trying to lean against the wind but failing, flung to earth, disoriented. On his knees, his arms folded over his head, he prayed for another streak of lightning. It came, and he glanced up. Only a hundred feet to go. He'd make it now. This must all be part of some plan, something preordained. He'd make it to the house, save the others, reveal everything. . . . He'd extended his hands, and after what seemed an interminable struggle, found them striking something solid. The side of the house. He flattened himself against it, gathering his strength. It was tempting to think of moving to his left, reaching the rear of the house, which he knew would be protected from the wind, and entering there. But he'd have to go in through the kitchen. . . . Shaking his head, he began making his way to the right, his body pressing against the wall. It wasn't quite as bad here. The wind's force wasn't quite as strong along the immediate side.

Then as he drew up to the corner of the house, the wind caught him and threw him back, slamming him to the ground. Trying to rise, he was thrown again, even more savagely this time. As he struck the earth, he felt something in his left shoulder give. A muscle had torn, or perhaps even a bone had shattered. He shrieked his pain and frustration, then rolled over onto his stomach and slowly, carefully, fought his way back onto his feet. All sense of direction lost, he simply headed into the wind, hoping he was right, praying for another flash of lightning.

The accumulation of pain from his nose, his hand, his shoulder, was nearly unbearable. He was almost beyond caring. And then he saw it. A faint glow to his left, the dim outline of a window. He was at the front of the house!

He staggered on toward where he thought the steps should be. As he did so, he squinted back over his shoulder toward the window. Was it too late? Was he walking into an even greater horror than he'd left behind . . . ?

There was no one at the window. *Doesn't mean anything, of course.* No reason why anyone should be at the window. Still, he felt fear creep into him, fear so great that his pain was almost forgotten. He forced himself to stumble on. He was at the steps now.

There was a flash of lightning. Something to his right moved. He turned.

It was very, very quick. His eyes widened in horror, his arms jerked upward protectively. . . . And then he was on a voyage, a journey, headed toward a warm, soothing light, a light of purity and peace. . . . He felt none of it, none of it at all.

14

The three of them had watched as Buddy and Tim left. Then they turned toward each other. "Hope I haven't led you astray," Sam said quietly.

"At the moment, I don't care," Karen told him. "All I want to do is revel in this silence, this blessed silence."

Sam was hefting the pick that had been left behind. "This is a pretty good weapon," he murmured, "but I'd like a backup. Look," he went on, "there's a big butcher knife in the kitchen. I'd like to go after it now, while it's quiet."

Karen and Eve looked stricken. "You're not going to leave us?" Karen gasped.

"No," he answered quickly, "I want you to come along with me. One of you can hold the door and the lantern. The other can keep an eye out behind us. It'll just take me a second," he urged. "It's right on the counter."

The two women exchanged glances. "You really feel you must?" Eve murmured, like a small girl asking a parent if it was an absolute necessity that she go to an event she dreaded.

"I know it'd make me feel a whole lot better," Sam told her.

Eve nodded. "All right."

Sam slid the easy chair out of the way and the three of them filed through the barricade. In the dining room they halted at the kitchen door. Sam motioned Eve to watch the rear. Then, as she turned her back to them, he pushed the door inward, let it swing back, and caught it with his hand. He motioned Karen to hold it with one hand and raise the lantern with the other.

As the lantern's feeble light washed over the gloom, Sam carefully, quietly, stepped down into the room. From the corner of his eye he saw the two bodies sprawled on the floor. The doors to the back kitchen and to the stairs stood half open, suggestive of terrors lurking a step or two beyond. He turned toward the counter.

His heart sank.

He glanced to the left, to the right, and ran his hand over the counter on the chance that the dim light had obscured it.

It wasn't there.

A vein in his temple began to throb. There was a knife holder on the wall in front of him. He reached for one of the knives, glanced at its blade, replaced it, and drew another. This one he kept. Very deliberately, he turned and went back up the stairs. The house was completely still.

Taking the door from Karen, he let it slowly close. Then he nodded, and the three of them made their way back to the living room.

After he drew the chair in, he laid the knife down on the table. Even as bad as things had been, even as bad as they might continue to be, Karen couldn't keep from smiling. "Just like a man," she said to Eve, pointing to the long, slender blade, "calling a carving knife a butcher knife."

He didn't correct her.

Eve moved to the couch. "Suddenly I'm so tired." She sighed.

"Just a minute," he told her, before she could lie down. "No sense in having the sofa face the fireplace anymore. Let's swing it in line with the wall, a few feet forward of it. Sort of give us a second line of defense. Something for you two to scoot behind while I see what I can do with the pick and"—he tried to smile—"my butcher knife."

When they were done and Eve had tucked herself into a corner of the couch, a thought came to him. Seizing the lantern and the remaining candle, he climbed over the furniture and strode to the center of the room, where he'd spotted a hook he could hang the lantern on. He placed the candle on a nearby shelf.

"That way," he explained as he returned, "if

we *should* have any visitors, we'll be able to see
them a whole lot better than they can see us."
Then he saw that he had only one listener. Eve
was asleep, her small form huddled at one end of
the long couch.

They stood and looked at each other with
small, sad, exhausted smiles. Karen took hold of
his sleeve and drew him down with her onto the
opposite end of the couch. "Let's talk. While we
can," she said.

The sight of Eve, so peaceful, so relaxed, served
to relax him, too. He stretched, and felt the tension begin to fade. It may be all right now, he told
himself. It may be all over with.

"The yearbook. The times I've had it out lately
. . . Each time I kept staring at the cover you did
for it." They were seated side by side, a few
inches apart, each staring straight ahead.

"I liked that one." He nodded. "Liked that one
a lot. Just brush and ink. Did it like that—whack,
whack, whack. Then I tried to see if I could do it
better. You know, being that good, but only the
first one, it figured I had a chance to improve it.
Tried it three or four more times. Didn't come
close."

"It was the whole school—in just a few lines,"
she murmured.

"Yeah. That was one I was proud of. That was
one I was glad I did."

As they sat in their barricaded corner, almost
completely sunken in shadow, Karen suddenly

realized that she was no longer afraid. She leaned against Sam, and it seemed to be just the way it had been in the old days. For the first time that evening she could smell him, could breathe in that fresh, strong scent that had intoxicated her so long ago. "You were so talented," she murmured. "You were such a good artist. Did you ever do anything with it? *Did* you ever go to Mexico?"

He nodded.

"So you did go." She smiled, almost dreamily. "It sounds so romantic, an artist in Mexico."

There was a slight sound, and he listened for a moment. Then, satisfied it had just been the house adjusting itself, he answered, "I thought so, too, for a while. Living in an adobe hut, cooking my own meals over an open fire, hauling in the water I needed. Learning a new language . . ." He put his arm around her. "And the painting— the colors . . . the colors of the sea, of the mountains. Mexico is very beautiful."

She nodded. "I've never been there. I wish I had gone. With you."

A wave of sadness passed through him. This night would soon be over. Things would be the same again, the same as they always had been. And yet . . . In the midst of the sadness, he suddenly realized there was a flicker of hope. "I could have been good," he told her. "*Would* have been. But it was all unreal, you see."

"Unreal?" She looked up at him for the first

time since they'd begun speaking, her eyes large, her lips half parted.

"All the poverty," he told her. "Of course I'd seen poverty before, God knows. I even saw enough of it in Everton . . . the old mill section. . . . But Mexico was something else."

He shook his head, as if seeing it all again. "Somehow, the dimension, the magnitude, of the misery, was so overwhelming that there was a kind of unreality to it—too much for my mind to register. Then I got called back to New York. A family thing. And while I was there I realized what I'd been seeing every day in Mexico. It finally sank in." He looked down at her. "I never went back."

"I don't understand," she told him.

"Painting no longer made sense. It was an indulgence, meaningless, vapid. I left all my paints and most of my clothes in that little hut. For all I know, they're still there."

"You're a man for surgical leave-takings," she told him quietly.

He winced. "I had to go," he told her, "after we got out of school. I was afraid that if I stayed . . ."

"That you might find yourself marrying me. And turning into what Buddy turned into."

He was silent.

"All right," she said, changing the subject, "after Mexico, what? All-out altruism?"

He laughed softly, ruefully. "Close, very close.

Went to work for a charity in Boston. Stayed there five years."

"What happened? Another surgical leave-taking?"

"Something like that. Noticed nothing I was doing really seemed to help anyone. It was all bureaucratic, all meaningless, too much money being paid to people at the top. So," he continued, self-mockingly, "I took the next step. Tried truth. Got a job as a reporter."

"Any better?"

"Marginally. Took me longer to catch on. Was there nearly seven years. Quit just before I came here."

"Just before . . ." She looked up at him. "When you leave here, do you know what you'll be doing, where you'll be going?"

He shook his head.

"All right," she said, snuggling against him. "Take me there with you. Wherever it is."

His smile was gentle, a little sad. "You've had a tough night," he told her.

"I'm serious, Sam," she insisted, her voice almost matter-of-fact. "I'm not suggesting you marry me or anything like that. We've been apart too long. But we could just try it for a while, see how it goes. . . ." She glanced up at him. "Or was all of that over for you a long time ago? Is that really why you left without saying good-bye, without even warning me you were going?"

"No." He shook his head. "It's not over. It's

never been over. That's why I never told you. Because I knew if you said one word, I'd have stayed."

"But after Mexico failed . . . why didn't you come back?"

"It was too late. You were married." He looked down at her. "You're still married."

She shook her head. "It's over. It's been over for a long time. It took tonight to make me realize it, but it's very clear now." Her voice filled with conviction as the thought came to her. "You know, like your time in Mexico, the way you didn't realize how bad things were there till you went away; had a new perspective . . . It's been the same tonight for me. I needed to pull away enough to see it. I needed this night of horror to finally make it clear. . . ."

"You could be seeing it all wrong," he said, "the abnormality of it . . . It could change come the dawn."

"Let me decide that," she told him. She turned so that she was half pressed against him. "Oh, Sam, I'm so happy. And it's made me so sleepy. Suddenly, so sleepy. Would you give me a kiss now, before I go to sleep? Just one kiss, a small one, one I can take with me into my dreams?"

He bent toward her, and softly, gently, brushed her lips with his. The sadness in him welled, the tiny light of hope flickered out. He found himself wishing the dawn would never come; hoped that she at least would live to see it.

* * *

Karen was in a place she'd never seen before, a place where she immediately sensed she belonged. She knew that inside her a child was growing; could feel its sweetness radiating inside her. She was walking near a cliff, staring into the rich blue of the sky, and the clouds, white as cotton balls, that dotted it. Somewhere, out of sight, just beyond the rise, Sam was seated beside a hut, painting. She was carrying flowers; she'd strew their petals over his lean naked body. She was very, very happy, happier than she'd been in a long, long time. . . .

Then something was wrong. She could hear the door of the hut flapping, flapping. . . . The sky was becoming dark, and she felt wind whipping at her skirts, lashing her face. She tried to call out, but the wind choked off her voice. She hurried to the rise, unable to breathe, her heart swelling in her breast, choking her. . . . But then she couldn't find the rise; found herself instead staggering through a jungle, sharp leaves and vines tearing at her, flaying her.

She was running from a horror, and yet at the same time running *toward* it. She felt fear cleaving into her like a spike, driving deep into her mind, her soul. . . . Then there he was . . . *Sam*. Blood was pouring from his mouth, streaming from his eyes. He leapt toward her; seized her; began to shake her. . . .

15

She awakened. Someone was shaking her. The light was strangely different, and the noise was incredible. The storm had returned, and there was something else. . . . "Wake up, wake up," Sam whispered urgently. "There's someone at the door. I've got to see who it is."

Eve was already awake, on her feet, and staring uncertainly at Sam. Sam handed Karen the knife. "Better you two have it. Just in case. Get down behind the couch, both of you." He waited until they obeyed, then left.

Karen's fear overwhelmed her now. Suddenly living meant so much more than before. She desperately wanted to live now that she had Sam. They could go away together, live together, have a child. . . . She heard the frantic banging on the door, then Sam's voice.

She waited, her eyes on Eve, seeing her fear reflected there. *I'll never see Sam again*. She knew that now.

And then she heard his voice again, this time shouting to them. "It's all right! It's all right! It's Buddy!" She began to sob, then fought it back. Unsteadily, she rose from the couch.

She saw now why the light was so strange. The last candle had burned out. There was only the lantern, and it seemed more feeble than before. In the dying light there was a moment when, as they entered, she couldn't tell the two men apart.

As Buddy came closer she drew back in horror. His face and hands were streaming with blood. He seemed to have aged ten years. He was fighting for words. "Where's Tim?" he finally gasped. "Did he make it back?"

Mutely they shook their heads.

Sam was soaked through; the storm had grown so fierce that Sam had been drenched in the instant he'd opened the door. He looked almost as shaken as Buddy. Karen's heart sank. Was he thinking the same thing she was? "I don't understand. Why isn't Tim with you?" she asked, barely able to get the words out.

"We got split up. Running, trying to find a way out before the storm reached us, I suppose I forgot I was faster than he was. Then it hit. No way I could find him after that. It's a nightmare out there. Far worse than before."

Karen breathed easier. That was all it was,

then. Tim was out there somewhere in the storm. Maybe he'd taken shelter, or was still fighting his way back to the house. . . .

Buddy was shivering. He still had on the borrowed clothing, which ran with water. "My own clothes must be dry by now. Drier than this, anyhow." He found them and began to strip, making no move to hide his nakedness; there was only Eve to consider now, and as the night had advanced, such niceties had become almost laughable. Besides, in his state, he probably wasn't even thinking . . .

"You're so cut up, so bloody," Karen said, feeling she should go to Buddy, minister to him, but unable to do it. "What happened?"

"All sorts of things flying around out there," Buddy gasped, still recovering. Fully dressed now, he fell onto the couch exhausted. "I was afraid I'd be blinded." He turned toward Sam. "Looked like you locked the door behind me. Do you think you should unlock it? In case Tim turns up, I mean. I had to knock for a hell of a long time."

"Took me a while to wake up, I guess," Sam said quickly. "Doubt if any of us'll fall asleep now. I won't, anyway. I'll have no trouble hearing him."

Buddy nodded wearily. "You're probably right. You were right about the storm." He turned to Karen. "He's right about a lot of things, isn't he?"

The question was enigmatic, and so was Buddy's tone. She looked away, unable to answer.

"There're four of us here now. We should be safer," Eve suddenly said, but the look in her eyes belied the words. Karen found herself shivering.

A silence fell. Sam remained on his feet, pacing, then stopping and standing motionless, facing the center of the room. As if he were *waiting,* Karen thought. There were four of them now, just as Eve had said. Buddy was at least as strong as Sam. But somehow she'd felt safer before Buddy's return. *It must be the nightmare. It must have shaken me.* She kept thinking of Tim, picturing him lying dead, butchered like the others. *Don't be absurd,* she told herself angrily. He's still alive. Probably dreaming up a wisecrack even as you're thinking about him, working on the words he'll greet us with when he turns up at the door. He'll be back . . . any minute now.

She thought back to those moments before she'd fallen asleep. It all seemed dreamlike now, unreal. . . . Was Sam right? Would everything be the same again when the dawn came, when they were safe? She could feel it slipping away from her, receding . . .

No. She couldn't let that happen. This awful night had revealed the truth. She stood, and moving resolutely to Sam, put her arm around his waist. "Say something to comfort me," she said, knowing that behind her Buddy was watching.

Sam was about to speak when a noise caught his

attention. He put a finger to his lips, cautioning them all to silence. They all heard it now. Tap . . . rub. Tap . . . rub. It was coming from the window nearest the fireplace. They stood stone-still as he slid over the table and took the lantern down. Tap . . . rub. Tap . . . rub. Tap . . . rub. Sam slowly crossed the room and held the lantern close to the window.

Eve cried out, then threw herself against Buddy. Karen felt herself slowly sinking into a deep black hole. Tim's face was pressed against the window, swaying back and forth, slapping against it, rubbing against it. But only Tim's face. Below it, there was nothing but a thin black pole. . . .

Karen flickered into consciousness as they carried her to the couch. But as soon as her body sank into the softness of the cushions, she fell into a deep, dreamless sleep. When she awoke, it was daylight. The storm was over. The air was chill. Before she could stop herself, she glanced toward the window near the fireplace. Someone had drawn the shade. *So she hadn't dreamt it.* Sam was standing near the barricade of furniture. Buddy and Eve were awake, too. "How long has it been light? How long has the storm been over?"

"Some time now," Sam told her quietly. "Ended about dawn."

"Why didn't you wake me?"

"No reason to. Wanted to give whoever it was a chance to get away."

Her hand went to her throat. "You think he's gone?"

Sam shrugged. "Even if he's not, he won't have the cover of darkness. We'll be all right."

She turned toward Buddy. What had happened between her and Sam seemed so long ago . . . and Buddy was her husband. She'd never seen him look so lost. How terrible he must feel, how guilty. Did he blame himself for losing Tim, for not being there to protect him? A wave of sympathy surged through her.

And yet she found she couldn't reach over to touch him; couldn't even find anything to say to him. She saw that Eve was watching, her eyes curious . . . and sad. Eve had a good marriage. She probably assumed everyone did. In any event, everyone like Buddy and her, who had admitted no problems to anyone, not even to themselves . . . Until last night. And now the night was gone. Soon they'd be stepping out into daylight. Soon she'd have to walk away with one of them, Buddy or Sam . . . and more and more she feared that it wouldn't be Sam.

16

"*My God!*"

Eve's cry was almost simultaneous with the banging on the door. It was frantic, loud, repeated, *mad*. All the terror she'd felt before, Karen realized, hadn't prepared her for this moment. Then there was the sound of glass smashing, and she found herself running with the others, into the hallway.

She stared at the tall, narrow stained-glass window beside the front door. One of its panes had been shattered. A bloodied hand was reaching through it, fumbling for the lock.

Sam leapt forward. In one motion he seized the hand and yanked it so that whoever was behind the door was drawn tight against the outside wall. "I've got him!" he yelled. "Open the door! He won't be able to attack while I'm holding him!"

The cry was meant for Buddy, but one glance told Karen and Eve it was up to them. Buddy was immobile, his eyes staring, his face ashen. He seemed paralyzed.

Karen rushed into the living room and seized the long, thin-bladed knife. Then she ran back, and with Eve, sprang for the door. She turned the lock. Then, together, she and Eve swung the massive door open.

What she saw robbed Karen of her speech.

"It's all right, Sam," Eve gasped. "It's all right. He's—he's badly hurt."

He was a small man, thin, and he was bleeding badly. The desperate gaze in his eyes was supplicating. Sam had released his hand, and now he was slowly collapsing against the side of the house, sliding down the wall.

Sam reached him before he collapsed onto the porch. Sweeping him up in his arms, he carried him inside and laid him down on the couch. Quickly, expertly, he unbuttoned the man's overcoat, then the white dress-shirt underneath. The two women recoiled as they saw the gash across the man's chest.

He was obviously in agony, but as Sam tended him, his eyes silently spoke his gratitude. Suddenly he recoiled, and terror spread across his face.

"Please!" he cried. "Please don't do any more to me!"

He was looking at Buddy.

Turning to the others, he implored, "Who are you, why did you do this?"

Sam's eyes were on Buddy. "You did it," he told him.

Buddy had followed them only a few steps into the living room. "No. No. don't you *see*?" he gasped. "He's the one. The one who killed all the others. All those back there, upstairs . . . Matt . . . Tim . . ."

Karen shuddered. She'd been holding the man's hand, trying to comfort him. He'd seemed too small, too vulnerable. . . . But if it had been he . . . then why was he here now, obviously a victim of the same kind of attack? Had Tim fought back, struggled with him? That must be it. . . . But then she glanced at Sam and saw the way he was looking at Buddy.

Sam turned back to the man. "You were one of the musicians, weren't you?" he asked gently. "At the reunion last night. In the gym?"

The man nodded feebly.

Sam turned toward the women. "I thought I recognized him. The band was still in the gym when we left. There's no way he could have gotten here ahead of us; killed those people . . . We left ahead of him. No one passed us on the road." He turned back to the man. "What happened?" he asked him softly.

Karen looked up at Buddy. He was shaking his head, back and forth, slowly, as if he were in shock. He looked sixty.

The musician's voice was a moan; fragments of sentences jerked out of him. "Bridge out . . . didn't see . . . grabbed floating tree . . ." He shook his head as if trying to summon up strength; managed to gasp out, "Thought storm over . . . saw lights here . . . headed toward . . . then it hit again . . ." He closed his eyes.

"Then the storm hit again," Sam encouraged him. "Go on. Don't stop now."

"Rain, wind . . . terrible . . . thought I'd never get to house. Then . . ." The look of terror reappeared in the dying man's eyes. "Lightning . . ." His eyes turned to Buddy. "Saw him . . . had ax . . . man on ground, hitting him . . ."

"Tim. He was hitting Tim," Sam interrupted. Then, "Yes, go on."

"Saw me . . . I started to run, slipped . . ."

"And then he attacked you. Left you for dead," Sam prompted him.

The man had closed his eyes. When he reopened them, their light seemed dimmer. He nodded. "Hid till morning . . . saw them"—he nodded toward the two women— "through window . . . Thought safe now." He shook his head feebly. "Why? Why'd you do this to me?"

Her brain swimming, Karen turned toward Buddy.

He was no longer there.

Frantically her eyes sought Sam's. She'd thought the nightmare was over. Instead, every-

thing that had happened till now seemed only
like the prelude: a prelude to total madness.
Buddy the murderer? It made no sense. He
hadn't been anywhere near this house until the
seven of them had driven here. She was certain of
that. The two of them had been together virtually
every moment yesterday. And Sam had said the
blood was fresh. Buddy couldn't have done it. Of
course he couldn't. Yet . . . this man seemed so
sure . . . but it had been night . . . the killer
could have been someone who looked like
Buddy.

And yet . . . Buddy . . . the way he'd
looked. And now he was gone, vanished. "For
God's sake," she breathed, "what does it mean?"

Sam shook his head. Eve looked stunned. The
man groaned, and they turned to him. But his
eyes flicked open for just an instant, then closed
again. As they did, Sam leapt to his feet.

Buddy was back.

He was on the other side of the now partly
opened barricade. He was holding an ax. One
look at his face and Karen knew the dying man
had been telling the truth, that somehow—in
some unfathomable way—what was impossible
was *so.*

When he spoke, his voice was calm, dispassionate. "I'm sorry," he said. "I didn't think I'd have
to kill you, too."

Karen shook her head. "It can't be," she cried.
"You couldn't have killed those people."

Buddy smiled a little. The smile was sad, haunted. "Not the people who lived here, no."

"I don't understand."

"Neither do I," he answered, still holding the ax, not moving. "I've never understood. I wasn't that kind of person. I'm not. Not even now. Not really. And I might never have been . . . if it hadn't been for Raymond."

Raymond. Wild-eyed, Karen glanced at Eve. So Eve had been right. There *had* been something after all, something wrong about Raymond. It might *not* have been a suicide. "Raymond," she gasped, her voice breaking. "What about Raymond?"

"There were things about Raymond. Terrible things." Buddy shook his head as if he still wasn't able to believe any of it. "I didn't know at first, of course. I just wanted to help him. I used to feel so sorry for him. . . . People made fun of him, mistreated him, snubbed him, ignored him. Exactly the opposite of the way I was treated. I'd always felt . . . privileged. You know that, Karen. Because of that I felt I owed something to people who weren't as fortunate as I was . . . who didn't have what I had; couldn't get what I could. . . . So I tried to do good things, helpful things for them . . . whatever I could. And by trying to help . . ." He jerked the ax and shrugged, his eyes bitter.

"Raymond *was* evil," Eve muttered feverishly. Naked pain stamped itself on Buddy's face.

"Yes." He grimaced. "It took me a while to realize. . . . But by then I was caught up in it. . . . There were things he did, things he thought of . . . They never would have occurred to me, *never* . . . Things I never would have realized were a part of me . . . because they were so subterranean, so dark, so far removed from what I thought I was. . . . I could have lived my whole life never knowing. But"—his voice faltered—"he . . . opened them up. He knew how to unlock things. No. He didn't *know* anything. He just did it naturally, without having to think about it, to plan. . . . Because that's what he was."

"And then he tried to blackmail you. Because of . . . because of what he'd unlocked." Eve's voice rang out, very sure, very positive.

Buddy nodded. "My whole life—everything I was. He had the power to destroy it, to demolish every last part of it—all by telling what he'd persuaded me to do, revealing it."

"But blackmail wasn't enough for him," Eve went on, caught up in it now. "You knew what he was like. No matter what you gave him . . . Sooner or later it wouldn't be enough. He was too evil for that. You knew a day would come when it would be all over for you. He'd expose you. No matter what you offered him. Because that's how deep his evil ran."

Buddy barely acknowledged her. "I knew I had to kill him. Before it was too late. Not that I allowed myself to think I'd do it. I kept telling myself that I couldn't. But there was another part of me that . . . All along, it *knew.* I invited him to come with us that night. I told myself it was because I wanted to help him, make him feel included. But a part of me knew. Knew I was hoping that somehow I'd get him alone, get him in a situation where . . ."

"The game of hide-and-seek," Eve said.

"Yes. The game of hide-and-seek. We were all supposed to stay inside the lodge. You remember. I knew Raymond. I knew he wouldn't obey the rules. He found pleasure in not obeying rules, in breaking them and not being caught." Sweat was beginning to break out on Buddy's forehead. "I followed behind him. Without letting him know, of course. And I was right," he continued, his face haggard. "I was right. He went out through a window. The one I guess Matt had opened up before the rules got changed. Out of the window, out of the house. He was going to stay there till everyone else had been caught, and then sneak back in. The winner."

"And you followed him," Eve said.

"Yes. I followed him. He didn't see me. I came up behind him."

"And struck him with something. Knocked him unconscious," Eve prompted.

"No. That might have left marks. I knew the town cops were idiots, but they weren't quite that stupid. So I strangled him."

"And then you hanged him. Hoped no one

would be suspicious enough to notice the finger marks."

"Yes. I hanged him. But the finger marks . . . I didn't know about that. I wasn't aware there'd be any difference. What did I know about murder? It wasn't till years later . . . reading about other incidents . . . that I realized how lucky I'd been."

"Lucky," Karen whispered, incredulous.

Buddy sagged. "Yes. Lucky. Not to be caught because of an oversight. That was my luck. My only luck, since then. No other luck since. Because of what I did, of course. It has to be that. I've never been free of it. Not for a day. Hardly even for a night. The dreams . . . waking in the dead of night . . ."

"So last night you suggested we visit Raymond's grave. Maybe hoping somehow that visit might allow you to lay it all to rest," Sam suggested, trying to keep Buddy talking, trying to buy time.

"No." Buddy shook his head impatiently. "I didn't suggest it. I don't know who did. But . . . but I did hope that maybe . . . What you said . . . that maybe I would be able to put it behind me. But of course I couldn't."

"Did you plan to kill us . . . from the start?" Karen asked, overwhelmed by the shock and the horror of what she was hearing. All these years, she'd never known, never suspected . . .

"No. No. Not till . . . not till we got here. Not

even then, not exactly. I mean, we found the bodies. Then Ruth kept making those sly remarks about Raymond, like she *knew* something. And then, just before she went upstairs . . . that last time . . . when she said it had been murder . . ."

"That's when you decided." Eve nodded.

"No. You don't understand," he cried, "I *never* decided. I kept telling myself I wouldn't *do* anything. You see, the thoughts kept coming to me, but I kept pushing them away. . . . All right, yes, I did think that if I could kill . . . the ones I was afraid might remember . . . kill them the same way the people in this house had been killed . . . then no one would ever guess. But it was only a thought. I saw the ax in the back kitchen. I threw it out in the rain, to keep it from tempting me. But all of you kept on about Raymond, going back over it again and again . . . I kept seeing the ax out there in the storm, kept telling myself I wasn't going to do anything. Until I found myself doing it. And then, just like it had been with Raymond, I knew that I'd planned to do it all along."

"My God," Karen breathed. "And in time you'd have killed all of us."

"No," Buddy cried, and then, after a pause, "Maybe. Yes. I don't know." His face was tortured. "I . . . I had to get a fresh start. Don't you see? What I did with Raymond, what I did to him, that wasn't me. I *know*. Because I was never like that again. But I *did* meet him, and then it was all over. . . . It all went wrong after that. . . ."

He shook his head in anguish. "Straight A's. That was all I knew. All I'd ever known. Remember? That photographic memory of mine? One read-through and I had it in my head, no matter what it was. But that began to fade. . . . My first days in college I realized I was losing it. For the first time I had to struggle for grades . . . cram . . . cheat." He glanced at Karen. "Had to lie about my marks. I didn't get the grades in college you thought I did."

His eyes left her and seemed to retreat into the past. "Then all the jobs that didn't work out. For no reason that I could see. I never told you how humiliated I was, having to come back and take over the business, hoping that would be the answer. And then seeing that drain away, too, year after year.

"All because of Raymond. And I'm still young, don't you see? There's still a chance for me. If I can put all this behind me, know I don't have to worry anymore about being caught . . . Because it's not who I am. You understand that, don't you, Karen? You grew up with me. . . . I'm not that kind of person; never would have been . . . if I hadn't met Raymond. . . ."

While Buddy was speaking, Sam had unobtrusively laid his hands on the pick. Now he said, "Put down the ax, Buddy. Please."

Buddy shook his head. "No. I don't want to kill

you. Didn't want to, anyway. Because none of you really knew, not like the others. Tim came to my house; saw me with Raymond. I was afraid . . . with all of you going back again and again over the past . . . that somewhere along the line he'd remember.

"And the time Raymond fell off Matt's motorcycle . . . he was hitching a ride to my house. Matt might have known that; might have remembered. The rest of you didn't know anything. But I have to kill you now. The way it is now, you see, now that you all know." He began to move toward them.

"Don't," Sam told him. He raised the pick.

"Too late," Buddy said, already halfway through the narrow passage in the tangle of furniture.

"No," Sam insisted, maneuvering so that he was between Buddy and the others.

The ax flashed up and then down.

The pick crashed against the side of it, deflecting it.

Buddy backed up, renewed his grip, and then came at Sam again, changing the angle of the blade so that as Sam reacted, it tore into the shaft of the pick, ripping it out of Sam's hands.

The follow-through of the ax left Buddy open. Before the pick hit the floor, Sam was on him, grabbing for the ax handle.

Buddy's hands were at its base, Sam's higher up, the blade turned toward him, dangerously

near. Karen leapt to her feet and seized the
kitchen knife, then recoiled as the two men
crashed against the furniture near her.

Buddy's body pitched back, Sam following. An
instant later the ax flew free, slashing through the
air, then clattering onto the floor of the hallway.
Eve ran for it, grabbed it, then frantically scrambled back behind the barricade.

Buddy had torn himself from Sam and was at
the far end of the living room, his eyes frantically
seeking out something to use as a weapon. There
was a large brass ashtray on the bookcase to his
left. Before he could reach it, Sam was on him.

Karen stared down at the knife. The men were
struggling, their legs straining, as they leaned
into each other. Buddy was an open target. A
quick run toward him, a sudden thrust . . . But
she didn't move.

Then Sam slipped, and Buddy was on him instantly, his fist crashing into Sam's jaw. The sound
of Sam's head striking the floor was sickening.

Simultaneously, unaware of each other, Eve
and Karen broke from their frozen positions and
ran toward the men. Eve got there first. She
raised the ax, then brought the blunt side down
against the side of Buddy's head.

It was a glancing blow that barely stunned him,
but it was enough margin for Sam. Swiftly he
upended Buddy, scrambled after him, then fell
on him, aiming short, telling punches at his head,
one after the other, sharp, bludgeoning blows.

Very quickly, Buddy's arms fell to his sides and his head lolled helplessly.

Sam pointed to the barricade. "Get one of those chairs! Quick!"

Karen ran back, seized one of the heavy dining-room chairs, and returned with it. Sam lifted Buddy into the chair, standing behind him, pinning his arms. "Give me something to tie him with," he urged.

Karen was wearing a thin leather belt. She stripped it off and passed it to Sam, who promptly pulled Buddy's hands back and lashed the leather around them. Buddy was beginning to stir. Sam nodded toward Eve, who still had the ax in her hands. "Keep that ready, just in case," he told her. She moved nearer to Buddy as Sam hurried toward the kitchen.

When he returned, he was carrying several lengths of rope. Quickly and expertly he tied Buddy to the chair, secured his body, his legs, his arms, his hands. By now Buddy was fully conscious. He gazed at Karen, then glanced away as his eyes filled with tears.

Sam straightened up. "All right," he said. "We can leave him here like this. No way he can get out of that. Let's go."

Karen shook her head. "I can't," she told him.

Sam didn't understand. "I know you're his wife, Karen, but . . ." he began.

"It's not that." She indicated the dying man on the couch. "I can't leave him. Not the way he is."

"All right," Sam told her. "We'll stay till it's over."

"No," Eve urged him. "It's important that you get back and let people know what happened here. Important you do it as soon as possible. Besides, it's certain to be bad out there. Floods, roads blocked . . . It'd be easier for you alone. You're a climber, a runner. . . . Karen and I'll stay together. We'll be all right."

He glanced at Eve, then at Karen. "You're sure?" he asked. They nodded. "Okay," he agreed, "I'll try to get back to you as soon as possible." His eyes and Karen's locked. Then he bit his lip, looked away, and left.

17

Karen watched him go, then moved to the couch. The dying man's breathing had become more labored, more shallow. His eyes were closed. She placed her hand on his brow, hoping it might soothe him. It was all she could do for him now. She watched through the window as Sam's figure slowly receded down the steep driveway; watched till he was out of sight. She turned toward Eve. "It's almost over," she said. Then she cursed herself as she realized what those words could mean to Eve.

But Eve didn't seem to notice. All she said was, "Yes, I believe it is." In the gray morning light she looked very weary, very lost. Then something seemed to strike her, and the weariness was gone. As she spoke to Buddy her voice was clear and insistent. "I understand how you killed Tim.

Matt, too. It would have been easy in that storm, slipping away from us, coming up on him, then rejoining us. But Ruth—how did you kill Ruth?"

Buddy shook his head. "I didn't kill Ruth," he said.

The room suddenly seemed very silent. Karen glanced at Eve, then at Buddy. Her mind raced back—years, it seemed—to last night. Ruth had left the room, looking for aspirin; had gone upstairs. They'd been talking, then they'd heard her scream. Buddy had reacted first and was on his way up the stairs before the rest of them had left the living room. But Ruth had screamed *first*.

Eve's mind was working the same way. Ruth had screamed. Buddy had reacted. *I wasn't that far behind him. He couldn't have done it. There hadn't been time for him to do all that had been done to Ruth.*

Buddy began speaking again. "That was what gave me the idea, you see. I mean, the hatchet. It was just a few feet from her body. I realized—it must have all come to me instantly, but it seemed to go on forever—you know, the way it is when your car goes into a bad skid, time stretching out —I realized what that hatchet could mean for me. The killer's fingerprints. They had to be all over it. If I could hide it, use another weapon— then when everything was over, clean off what I'd been using and drop the hatchet beside the last body. . . ." The words poured out, as if somehow they could make things right. "There was a drawer underneath a closet—the passage beside the stairs—I dropped the hatchet into the drawer, then slid it closed."

Slid the drawer closed. *The sound of a drawer closing.* What she'd heard as she'd run up the stairs. Eve nodded slowly. She knew Buddy was telling the truth. She turned toward Karen. A frightening question had begun to form in her mind.

"Then"—Karen stammered— "then whoever killed those people . . . He was still in the house when we arrived. He was the one who killed Ruth."

Buddy stared at her. He said nothing.

"What about . . . about . . . Tim's head? Did you do that?" Eve asked, afraid of the answer.

Buddy shook his head. "Tim was dead when I left him. But his head . . . I didn't do that. I thought he"—he pointed to the dying man— "had done it. When I saw him out there. But obviously . . . he didn't."

"Then . . . then . . . *who?*" Eve gasped.

Buddy's voice was quietly sure. "Sam," he said. "It had to be Sam. Remember what I said last night? He was in the back kitchen . . . said he was . . . when Ruth was killed. But he was wet through. Claimed he'd seen someone outside just before that; had gone out in the rain . . . that that was why he was wet. But of course he'd killed Ruth, and then dropped from a window to the ground. Ran through the rain back to the kitchen."

Karen's head was swimming.

"No!" Eve cried. "He couldn't have done that to Tim! He was with *us* all night!" She turned to Karen, as if for confirmation.

Numbly Karen shook her head. When Sam had awakened her . . . Had he been wet then? Had he been wet through even before he'd opened the door for Buddy? She couldn't remember; wasn't sure. "You were asleep," she told Eve. "I was asleep. After Sam let Buddy in . . . I thought Sam was wet because of the rain coming in through the front door. . . ."

"Sam . . ." Eve whispered.

Buddy's voice was stronger now, and surer. "You've got to untie me. Don't you see? He'll be coming back. It's only a ruse, his leaving. He must have killed the others, too. Remember? He was so sure the blood was fresh. He'll be coming back to finish you off. Untie me."

Eve and Karen stared at him; began to understand what he was telling them. They turned toward each other. Behind them, the throat of the dying man began to rattle. . . .

Sam was near the end of the driveway, out of sight of the house. From the debris on the lawn it was obvious the water had already receded several feet. He moved further down the drive, one yard, two . . . Then the bottom flattened out, and he knew he was standing on the road. The water was six inches above his ankles. If he could stand the cold, he could keep to the road for much of the way. It might not take more than an hour to reach a highway, hitch a ride . . . might not take long to get out of here. He nodded to himself and then turned back toward the house.

His first steps were unhurried, deliberate; but as he advanced toward the house, they accelerated. Buddy tied up, just the two women . . . defenseless, for all purposes.

Karen and Eve. *Karen.*

Buddy was pale with fear. "Please. Please, release me. God, don't you see? He'll kill you two first. I'll be helpless. Watching . . . And then he'll come at me. . . . For God's sake, you can't do that to me. There's no way the two of you can stop him. But I can. You know I can. I'd have had him before if you hadn't . . . Please!"

The two women clung to each other for a moment, then separated. Each knew she couldn't afford tears; couldn't afford to break down; had to fight down the growing panic before it immobilized her.

Outside, Sam had it worked out. The butcher knife. The missing butcher knife . . . It would all be over soon. One way or the other.

Karen was stronger than Eve. She'd taken the ax. Eve was gripping the carving knife. "That's right," Buddy said to Eve. "Cut me loose."

Sam glanced at the sun-filled sky. How

strangely it was like any day, any ordinary day. . . .

They seemed to have been waiting for hours. Then, when they heard the steps on the front porch, Karen realized too late: They hadn't locked the door behind Sam after he'd left; had seen no reason to. She glanced at Eve. *We'll get out of this. Dammit, we'll get out of this.*

They tensed. The front door was opening. Then, slowly, very slowly, he entered the hall, neared the entrance to the living room . . . and stood there. The ax dropped from Karen's hands.

The dream was over. All the fragile hopes . . .

Sam was soaked with blood. Karen raced to him and threw her arms around him, sobbing.

His voice was so weak she could barely hear. "Suddenly occurred to me. Buddy'd used an ax on Matt and Tim. Ruth and the family had been killed with a *hatchet*. And when Buddy saw Tim's head he nearly collapsed, too. Wouldn't have reacted that way if he'd done it. Started shaking because he knew the killer had to still be here."

He jerked his head in the direction of the front yard. Seeing the sudden fear in Karen's eyes, he tried to say something but failed.

His body was becoming too heavy for her. Wordlessly she glanced at Eve, who hurried over. Together they lowered him to the floor. "So strange," he said weakly. "So normal-looking." His eyes clouded, then for an instant as he gazed at Karen they grew unnaturally bright. He struggled to speak. But then his head rolled to one side.

They found a blanket and covered him with it, drawing it all the way over him. Buddy, still tied up, watched them, saying nothing, stunned by what he saw in Karen's face.

She rose and walked toward him, the ax in her hands. He closed his eyes as she strode behind him and stopped.

But she was checking the ropes. "They should hold." She nodded, then turned to Eve. "Let's go," she told her.

They moved together through the hall and out the front door, Karen with the ax, Eve with the knife. They stepped onto the porch, paused, and then started down the steps. Near the base of the stairs they halted. The rest of Tim was on the lawn to their left. Averting their eyes, they hurried down. Then, to their right, they saw him.

He was huddled against the wall of the porch. The two women understood now what Sam had meant. He was so terribly normal-looking. A young man, still in his twenties, baby fat filling out his cheeks, his hair curly and tousled. His eyes were a clear blue, his mouth small, with slightly parted pouting lips, showing very white teeth.

He was wearing a light-blue down-filled jacket and white corduroy pants. He was covered with fresh blood. Partially obscured by it was the older blood also spattered over his clothes. Karen thought she recognized him; had seen him somewhere, maybe at one of the stores in the mall . . . a clerk . . . harmless-looking. And no one would ever know why, she thought. The boy was dead. His eyes were open, and at first she'd thought he was alive, but now she could see. Sam had done his job. He'd come back to protect them, and he had. A bloodied butcher knife was still in the boy's hand. Sam's thumbprints were large blue marks on his neck.

The two women hurried past the dead body to the thinly graveled driveway. It was steep and rough, pitted with small gullies. As they descended, Karen felt an impulse to turn and take one last look at the house. She fought it for an instant, then shrugged and glanced back.

Framed by the dazzling blue of the morning sky, illuminated by a blindingly strong sun, it looked like an old farmhouse, of no particular character or distinction. It could have been a farmhouse anywhere, bland, run-down, uninteresting.

Beside her, Eve walked quickly, her stride shorter than Karen's. Except for the occasional sound of a bird, there was total quiet.

18

For a while, Buddy listened, straining to hear. If the killer was outside, waiting for them, if Sam hadn't finished him off . . . then it would all be over. *And if, somehow,* the killer didn't return to the house, he'd be free, free at last.

Except that he didn't want to be free. Not anymore. The obsession was gone now, all over with. But he could never be free, not from himself. Bad as it had been before, it would be worse now.

For years he'd meditated, trying to free himself of the guilt and the fear. It had worked . . . for an hour at a time; occasionally, at best, for part of a day. He'd become good at it; had learned to control his thoughts, his breathing, his pulse . . . his heart.

It might work, he told himself. He'd struggled against the ropes, but it was no good. He'd heard no screams. The women were probably getting away. They'd reach the town cops, tell them, and soon they'd be here, arresting him, bringing him into custody. The people in the town would find out, his brothers and sisters and aunts and uncles would find out . . . And he'd know they knew. Even if he never saw them again, refused all visitors, he'd know. . . . He couldn't stand that; couldn't stand the shame. . . .

What'll I try . . . slowing my heart to where it finally doesn't beat anymore, or making it accelerate until it goes berserk, bursts . . . ? The first. Everything I've learned has been to slow things down. I've gotten good at it, very good. Try that first. If it doesn't work, I can always try it the other way.

He began to clear his mind; started to force things away. . . . Soon his concentration was absolute, a long, narrow black corridor that ended in the steady beating of his heart. His mind reached out and pulled back, held the beat, then released it. Again . . . again . . . Only this time the wait for the beat that followed was longer. His mind pushed forward, holding it back . . . did it again . . . and again. Slowly, steadily, the beats began to slow. Then they began to falter. . . .

The two women neared the end of the driveway and stopped. Everywhere they looked they saw water. The area across the road was a tangle of fallen trees and shattered limbs. Glints of blue played on the water. "Look!" Eve cried.

Karen stared in the direction Eve was pointing. Something smooth and shiny was glowing just above the surface. "Isn't that the roof of your car?" Eve asked. Karen recognized the color. "The end of that, too," she said quietly. She knelt and dipped the tip of one finger into the water that stood near her feet. "Freezing," she told Eve. "But I think we're going to have to walk through it. I don't see any alternative."

Eve glanced up and down the property. She saw nothing that could be used for a raft. "I suppose we might find something in that garage or maybe by the shed. . . . But I don't want to go back," she said.

Karen nodded. She couldn't have done it, either. Carefully she placed one foot in the water. She was still on the driveway. She advanced three more feet and found the road. Her feet were already stinging from the cold. "Come on," she urged. "Maybe if we keep moving . . ."

It didn't help. The more they pushed through the water, the more painful it became. The cold was so intense it felt like fire, searing their feet, their ankles, the pain reaching all the way to the backs of their knees. They tried to avoid splashing, but invariably they did. Each time it happened, they flinched, stung by the icy water.

A bank of clouds began to fill the sky, covering the sun, and soon every part of them was chilled.

After a quarter of a mile they found they were clinging to each other as they walked, instinctively drawn toward the warmth of each other's bodies.

But still the cold crept further into them. They began to shiver, and then to sob. Once, simultaneously, they turned and looked back, as if even returning to the horrors of the house would be better than this. But they'd gone too far; the land was nowhere in sight.

"It's supposed to be over," Karen wept.

"It will be soon. It will be," Eve answered, desperately.

It wasn't easy to keep to the road. Often it was a tangle of debris, and when they'd made their way around it, they'd find they had strayed from their path. Using broken branches, they'd sound the water, tapping till they found asphalt. Eve began to moan. "You'd better go on without me. I can't take any more of this." Her teeth were chattering and her lips were blue.

"You can't quit. Look!" Karen urged, pointing. "We're coming to a rise. We'll be able to get out of the water, at least for a while. Come on!"

They began to run, heedless of the spray they caused; their quivering, blue-veined flesh couldn't be affected any further. Overhead a plane's engine sounded; it was the first hint they'd had that somewhere, not too far from them now, civilization continued. They looked at each other and laughed, hope beginning to fill them.

The water became shallower; soon the tops of their shoes began to show, and then, all at once, they found themselves free of the water. "Quick! Rub your legs!" Karen cried, bending down toward her own.

For nearly a minute they massaged their legs, but it seemed to do no good: Eve had become even paler, and Karen was shivering more violently than before. "No point in this," Karen finally decided. "We'll just have to keep going."

Eve nodded, too numbed to speak, and they began again, half running in an effort to warm up and end the hell their bodies were enduring. They reached the crest of the hill. Below them they saw the cemetery, and beyond it the place where the station wagon had nearly been swept off the bridge. There was nothing left of the bridge, and water was roaring several feet above where it had been. In despair they looked at one another. There was no way they could cross.

"I can't go back," Eve gasped weakly, "I couldn't survive it."

"This should be the last stretch of water," Karen said. "I think it's all high land after this. And houses shouldn't be too far away. We've got to find a place to cross."

They began climbing the hill that bordered the river. It was all cliffs and crags, blanketed by the ugly residue of the hurricane. After two hundred feet of scrambling through mud and debris and over the slippery rocks, Karen saw it, about twenty yards ahead of them. A large tree had fallen, bridging the swollen river. It was almost thirty feet above the madly rushing water. As Eve clambered up behind her, Karen wordlessly pointed it out. Her eyes wide, Eve took it in. The two shivering women pushed forward.

When they reached it they saw that the tree was more than two feet in diameter. The base stood near their feet, roots thrusting out in every direction. Their eyes traveled the length of the tree. The trunk was free of branches for ten feet or so past where it rested on the other side.

Their teeth chattering, their bodies shaking violently, the two women began to laugh, feeble titters at first, then giggles, then full-throated roars.

Each time they thought they'd conquered their laughter, they'd exchange glances and begin all over again. The agony had finally become absurd, the never-ending quality to it ultimately laughable. Finally, drained, Karen turned toward the tree, placed her arms around the trunk and tried to move it. It stood fast. "Help me," she told Eve. Together they tried to rock it. No results. "Seems safe enough." She shrugged, as if safety at this point was just barely worth considering. "Who goes first?"

"You," Eve said, and then, "No, never mind. I'll try it. Better *I* be the guinea pig." She hugged

Karen. "Wish me luck," she whispered, and then straddled the tree. Lying face down, she slowly began to pull herself along it.

Karen thought all her fear had long been exhausted. But as she watched Eve painfully, laboriously, make her way over the tree, she felt a chill that had nothing to do with her shaking body. The tree had seemed firm, but how could they be sure? They hadn't the strength to test it the way a man could have . . . the way Sam could have. At any moment it might suddenly start to slide, and there'd be nothing she could do about it. . . .

But as Eve inched along the tree it continued to hold firm. Like everything else that had been exposed to the storm, it was wet and slippery, and Eve was ill and cold and exhausted. At any moment she might find herself slipping, too weak to recover. The roar of the water seemed to grow louder, and Karen, unable to do anything, unable to help, began to cry, allowing herself, trying to relieve the terrible tension with tears.

And then Eve was across! Her feet touched down on rock, she pulled herself forward another few feet, then swung off the tree, turned, and waved to Karen.

Hope surged through Karen's body, warming her. Fearfully, eagerly, exultantly, she stretched out on the tree, slid her arms forward, and began to pull herself along. Immediately she understood why it had taken Eve so long to make her way across. The bark was rough, and it caught against her clothes as she tried to pull herself forward. It caught and tugged and jerked, keeping her slightly off balance everytime she moved. There was nothing to grip; she could only place her hands forward, press down, and pull, hoping her fingers wouldn't slip; and then when they did, her heart stopped as her body slid to the left or the right.

The further out she got on the trunk, the louder the roar of the water became. When she was halfway across, the sound blotted out everything else. She was afraid to raise her head, fearful it might cause her to lose her balance; her whole world had become only the few inches of striated gray-brown bark ahead and the explosion of the water beneath.

And then, miraculously, the roar of the water began to subside. Carefully, she looked up. Safety was only a few yards away. Eve was shouting encouragement.

Karen began to move more quickly. It was a mistake. One hand forward, then the next, placed carelessly. All at once she felt her hand lose its grip, and her body begin to slip. It was exactly like a nightmare, precisely like the dreams she'd had as a child, and then as an adult, feeling herself in that terrifying precariously balanced place between safety and utter destruction; uncertain if she had already gone past the point of no return.

Oddly, she felt no fear. Only sadness. She was

going to die now, just when it seemed that all the horror was behind her. . . . It seemed so wrong, so tawdry. To fail now, now when she was almost free . . . She'd hit the water, be carried along, dashed against rocks, the freezing temperatures penetrating the final, feeble warmth of her battered body. . . .

In a daze she felt something press against her shoulder, halting its downward slide, forcing it upward. Wild-eyed, she glanced up to see Eve in front of her, stretched along the trunk again, doing what she could to save her friend. "Come on! You can make it! You'll be all right!" Eve was shouting.

They were together in eternity. Then Karen felt her body move a fraction of an inch higher, her left leg lower, her right push back to grasp a higher portion of the trunk. Finally, one more tug and she had regained her balance.

Imploringly, she stared at Eve. She wasn't sure she could force herself forward.

"You can do it," Eve urged. "You *can*!" She reached forward, grasped Karen under the arms, then, very carefully, began to pull. Slowly, just barely, Karen inched forward. The movement was hardly measurable, but it was enough. Karen felt herself back in control. "Okay. I can do it now." She nodded. "Better if I do it myself."

Her gaze never leaving Karen, Eve slowly retreated as Karen began to inch her way forward. Then Eve's feet touched ground. Again she stretched out on the trunk and very carefully gripped Karen's jacket. Then one of Karen's feet dropped and she felt her toe touch something solid. She pushed her foot forward, groped, and found a toehold. Using it, she pushed along the tree, one foot, two, till there was only land beneath her. She slid off the tree, then collapsed against it, her arms wrapped around Eve.

Their clothes torn, their mud-caked hands and faces scratched and bleeding, they made their descent down the mountainside. When they reached the wet asphalt of the road, they impulsively embraced. "We made it," Karen sobbed. "We made it."

By now they were both barefoot, their coats and skirts in rags, but they didn't notice, intent only on what lay ahead. Twenty minutes went by.

Finally Eve gasped, "Look!" A few hundred yards down the road stood a house, and in the distance beyond it another, and then another.

Half laughing, half crying, they began running, supporting each other as they ran. As they neared the house, they began to veer off the road, angling toward it across the broad front lawn.

All at once they stopped. At first they saw just the one body. Then, as they walked slowly forward, the two others. A young man, a young woman, a small girl. Karen and Eve turned toward the house. Half its roof was blown away. There was no sign of life. The storm had wiped out the entire family.

"No more! No more!" Eve screamed, her face a distorted mask. Desperately Karen reached out and pulled Eve toward her, stroking her, crooning to her, pushing away her own despair as she strove to keep Eve with her, to prevent her from crumbling entirely, retreating irrevocably from the world. Karen shut her eyes tight, pressing Eve tightly, stroking, crooning . . .

Then she heard it, a sound so normal, it was jarring . . .

. . . the sound of a truck approaching. She opened her eyes and watched as it neared. Things would be all right now. It was all over. Everything was going to be all right. Eve was watching now, too.

The truck slowed to a halt. The door opened and a man stepped out dressed in a seaman's cap, faded jeans, and a worn leather jacket. He paused, then began moving slowly toward them. *It would be all right now, all right.*

He was very close now, only yards away, his ice-blue eyes focused hard on them. Something glinted in the sunlight. Karen glanced down. The man's arm hung alongside his body. There was something in his hand, something shiny. . . .